A Home Is to Share...
and Share...and Share...

Also by Judie Angell

DEAR LOLA
A WORD FROM OUR SPONSOR
THE BUFFALO NICKEL BLUES BAND
IN SUMMERTIME IT'S TUFFY
TINA GOGO
WHAT'S BEST FOR YOU
RONNIE AND ROSEY
SECRET SELVES
SUDS
FIRST THE GOOD NEWS

JUDIE ANGELL

*A Home Is to Share...
and Share...and Share...*

BRADBURY PRESS   NEW YORK

Bradbury Press
An Affiliate of Macmillan, Inc.
866 Third Avenue
New York, N.Y. 10022
Collier Macmillan Canada, Inc.
Manufactured in the United States of America
10 9 8 7 6 5 4 3 2
The text of this book is set in 12 pt. Baskerville.
Library of Congress Cataloging in Publication Data
Angell, Judie.
A home is to share . . . and share . . . and share . . . .
Summary: When the Muchmore children start taking in stray animals,
their parents are at first good-humored, but then the town animal shelter
closes, business booms, their parents become impatient, and the children
operate their haven in secret.
[1. Pets — Fiction.   2. Brothers and sisters — Fiction]
I. Title.
PZ7.A582Ho   1984   [Fic]   83-21356
ISBN 0-02-705830-1

To Roy Miles Cohen
with love

1...

Mrs. Muchmore heard the screen door open with the loud screechy-squeal it always made when someone was in a hurry. "Someone" was always Bucky.

"Bucky, don't let the door—"

Slam!

"—slam," Mrs. Muchmore finished.

Beverly "Bucky" Muchmore, twelve years old, red-faced, with damp brown curls sticking to her forehead, raced into the kitchen. Her mother, working at the kitchen table, put a finger down to keep her place in her pile of papers and waited until Bucky caught her breath.

"Mom, you've got to come right away—"

"Bucky—"

"Mom, you've got to. Please! Jeanette's there, she's waiting for you—"

Mrs. Muchmore jumped from her chair. Some of the papers went flying.

"Jeanette? Is she all right?" Jeanette was Bucky's sister, younger by three years.

"*She's* all right. *She's* fine. It isn't Jeanette, it's the dog!"

Mrs. Muchmore sat down again with a sigh. "The dog," she said, "is right here under the table." She bent down to pick up stray papers and stroked Calpurnia with her free hand.

"Not Cal*pur*nia!" Bucky said. "*Another* dog!"

"Now listen, Beverly," her mother said. "I've got all these bills to do—" she swept her arm across the table, "—and new orders to handle and I don't have time for you and your sister's—"

"No, Mom, this dog's in real trouble. People can wait to get their Venetian blinds, but this dog can't wait!"

Mrs. Muchmore ran the Nelkin Falls Venetian blinds business from their home. She looked down at her piled work.

"The dog will have to wait, Bucky," she said. "I couldn't be busier now."

"Look," Bucky said, tugging at her mother's sleeve, "she's down in front of the A and P. In the parking lot. And she's pregnant! She's going to give birth any second now! You have to come,

2

Mom, you have to! Jeanette is sitting with her while I get you."

"No, Bucky," Mrs. Muchmore said. "I'm working."

Bucky made an exasperated face and slapped at the side of her head with her palm. "I *knew* Jeanette should have come to get you! I *told* her! But no-oo, she had to stay with the dog. I couldn't *pry* her away from the dog. *I* could have stayed with the dog—"

"Aw, Bucky, it wouldn't have made any difference. I have work to do. See? Honest. Now go back and tell your sister—"

"Jeanette was putting cold compresses on her head. The dog's head, I mean. Mrs. Safer from the card shop was bringing out paper towels—"

"Now, Bucky, I am not running down to the shopping center now and I mean it. I have too much to do. And Harry's outside playing—"

"We'll bring Harry!" Bucky cried. Harrison Muchmore, the youngest, was six.

Mrs. Muchmore jabbed the air with her pencil. "Another stray—" she said. "Beverly Muchmore, I am *not* going to disrupt everything because of another one of these animals you kids are always dragging home. And that's final!"

. . .

"Where are we going, Mom?" Harry asked

3

as his mother stuffed him into the back seat.

"The shopping center," she grumbled. Bucky was already in the front passenger seat, wiggling and biting her lip.

"You'd better hurry, Mom, it might be too late."

"I'm hurrying, I'm hurrying, but I'm not going to have an accident. Strap your seat belts, kids."

Bucky clicked her belt into place and felt a drop of perspiration tickle her temple. She reached up with the hem of her T-shirt and wiped it.

"It's hot," she said.

"Mmmm . . ."

Bucky looked out her window at the huge maple trees along the side of the residential streets they passed. In summertime the maples were so full, trees from both sides of the street seemed to meet in the middle, blanketing out the sky for those passing underneath. Bucky liked that. It made her feel as if she were covered in a cocoon of leaves.

When they drove into the open again, she cried, "We're here!" and unsnapped her seat belt.

"We've still got three blocks to go, Bucky," her mother said, "so don't get out — we're still moving." She turned left at the old stone library. Bucky craned her neck as they pulled into the Nelkin Falls Shopping Center, but she could barely see Jeanette because a crowd of shoppers with carts had gathered around her.

Bucky was out of the car the second it stopped.

"Let us through, let us through," she said, pushing a path for herself, her mother and Harry. "Emergency help is here, let us through —"

"Oh, boy. What took you so long?" Jeanette asked, looking up. "She's going to die of heat frustration before she even gives birth!"

"*Pros*tration," Mrs. Muchmore corrected automatically and knelt down.

"I'm glad you came, Mom," Jeanette said, and her mother smiled and shook her head as she inspected the animal.

The dog was definitely pregnant. Her protruding belly heaved with tiny jerks from the puppies inside. She wore no tags, no collar.

"Hello, Goldie," Mrs. Safer called. "Going to take this one home, too?"

Mrs. Muchmore looked up. "Oh, hi, Marge. I guess so. At least for a while. Want a puppy?"

"No, thanks." Mrs. Safer frowned. "Poor thing. I wouldn't want to give birth in this heat. Honestly, isn't this July the worst? At least my shop's air-conditioned."

"Wish my house were," Mrs. Muchmore said. "Come on now, girls. If we're going to take her, let's get her into the car. Harry, you can help. I think she's got some time yet . . ."

. . .

2...

The Muchmores' basement was large. And cool. In hot weather the stone walls sweated with dampness. There was a washing machine and dryer under the stairs, and on the opposite wall, under a window, Mr. Muchmore kept a small workbench with tools hung from corkboard above it. The basement still contained Harry's old baby carriage and there were shelves for worn-out toys and books as well as skates, boots, bats and balls, most of which were not sitting on the shelves, but on the floor.

"Where should we put her?" Jeanette wailed. "There's no room . . ."

"We'll push some of this stuff away and make room," Bucky said.

"How about putting it back on the shelves?" Mrs. Muchmore said, but Bucky was busy planning.

"Harry, you get some rags," she said.

"Where are they?"

"In that pile," Bucky told him.

"No, that's our laundry," Mrs. Muchmore sighed. "The rag pile is over there, next to the workbench."

The girls cleared away some beach toys and chairs that had been stacked against a side wall, and there they made a small mound of the soft rags.

"Make it neater, Bucky," Jeanette prodded. "Like a bed. Put a pillow up here so she can lean."

Bucky clicked her tongue. "You want a lamp?" she asked. "So she can read?"

"I just want it nice," Jeanette said with a tentative smile. "She's pregnant and she's our guest . . . I want it nice."

"So she'll drop in here next time she's in Nelkin Falls," Mrs. Muchmore said. She bent down to stroke the dog's matted fur. "Okay. Let's give her a chance to cool off and rest, and then she gets a bath."

"A bath?" Jeanette looked worried. "Can you take a bath when you're pregnant?"

Her mother smiled. "Yes, my dear," she said, "you can certainly take a bath when you're pregnant." She looked down at the dog again. "She's nowhere near labor now. And she sure could use a good cleaning. She's really quite a mess."

Harry, who had been crouched next to the dog's belly, grinned up at them. "I can hear them in there," he said. "And I can feel them! Mom, I can *feel* them!"

"Maybe she'll be better-looking after the bath," Mrs. Muchmore said. "She's not the prettiest thing I ever saw . . ."

"Sh!" Bucky said. "She'll hear you."

Calpurnia lumbered down the basement stairs, sniffing.

"Kids, take Calpurnia out for a walk," their mother said, "so she won't bother this" — she shook her head — "dog."

. . .

Mr. Muchmore, home from work, heard the argument coming from the bathroom all the way to the front door.

"Don't *towel* her, Bucky, you'll *hurt* her!"

"No, I won't! You can't use a blow dryer on a dog! It'll *scare* her!"

"*You're* scaring her, not *me*! You're rubbing her too hard!"

"I am not!"

"Anyone home?" Mr. Muchmore called.

"*I* want to dry her! Let *me*!" Harry yelled.

"Hi there," Mrs. Muchmore said, coming to greet her husband.

"Don't tell me," he said. "Let me guess. Another animal."

"It's pregnant," his wife said.

"Didn't we agree—"

"—that now that we have only one dog and three cats we'd stop bringing any more home. Yes," she said. "We agreed."

"So here's another stray," he said.

"Here's another one."

He grunted. "Dog?"

"Dog. Ugly as sin. You wouldn't believe it. And absolutely no expression. Her eyes are glazed over. The poor thing must've been through the mill, Howard. Honestly, she has the personality of a bored guppy. Wait till you see her."

"I can wait."

"No. You can't. The kids've been crazy for you to get here. We cleaned her up. She's gone from gritty-black and muddy to scruffy-brown and dirty-white."

"Sounds like a real winner . . ."

"The kids love her."

"Of course they do. They've loved them all."

"*Now* look what you've done! You've *burned* her!" Bucky cried from the bathroom.

"*I* haven't burned her, you *poked* her too hard, Bucky!" Jeanette sounded near tears.

"Let *me*!" Harry wailed.

"Hey, hey!" Mr. Muchmore said from the bath-room doorway. "That poor thing may not bite you, but *I* might. Let's all calm down, okay?"

The three children stopped their battle at once and looked up at their father.

"Hi, Daddy . . ." Jeanette said.

"Hi, Daddy!" Harrison echoed.

"'Lo, Dad," from Bucky.

Mr. Muchmore looked down at the dog on the mat. She stared back at him listlessly. Heavy lids hung over rheumy eyes. Her fur was still matted in places and missing in places. One ear was chewed.

"Hello, girl," Mr. Muchmore said, kneeling down. He held out his hand. The dog made no attempt to sniff at it.

"What's your name, girl?" Mr. Muchmore asked.

Harry perked up immediately. "Sparky!" he cried.

His father turned from his kneeling position and looked at his wife. "Sparky?"

"Sparky!" Jeanette agreed happily.

The dog closed one eye.

"Sparky," Bucky said, nodding. "Perfect."

. . .

It was Harry's job to set the table with his father each night—a short, quiet time for the men to be together at the end of the day.

Carefully, he folded the paper napkins into triangles.

"That was an interesting name you picked for the dog, Har," Mr. Muchmore said with a smile.

"Yeah . . . good name," Harry said. "We can keep her, can't we, Daddy?"

"Well, Harry, I wouldn't count on that . . ."

"Oh, please? I want to have puppies again, Daddy. Wouldn't it be nice to have puppies again?"

"Harry, you gave your mom four napkins."

"Oh. Sorry. Well, but aren't puppies fun, Daddy?"

"Well . . ."

"They're so cute . . . and their little eyes are closed for so long . . ."

"Harry?"

"Huh?"

"Forks."

"Forks?"

"We need them. To eat with."

"Didn't I put down the forks?"

Mr. Muchmore shook his head.

"I'll get 'em," Harry said.

"Good idea."

"Daddy, puppies are too little to really be much trouble, aren't they?"

"Get the forks, Harrison," his father said.

.   .   .

The evening was muggy, and Mrs. Muchmore served cold cuts and potato salad. Still, everyone was more thirsty than hungry and the punch and lemonade were the first to go. Every once in a while, Mr. Muchmore would mutter, "Sparky," and shake his head.

"Opal and Ruby *love* Sparky," Harry piped. Opal and Ruby were two of the Muchmores' three cats. "But Fraidy is under the bed . . ."

"Fraidy is always under the bed," Bucky said and nudged her brother in the ribs.

"But Calpurnia is wonderful!" Jeanette said quickly. "She likes having a new friend."

"Calpurnia," Mrs. Muchmore remarked, "growled twice and has been in the back yard with her nose between her paws ever since Sparky came upstairs for her bath."

"Oh, but she'll get over that so fast," Jeanette said. "She's been lonely, being the only dog. Now she'll have someone to play with." Her parents still didn't seem as enthusiastic about Sparky as she hoped, so, thinking fast, she kept talking. "Just like Bucky was lonely when she was the only kid. That's why you got me and Harry, right?"

Mr. Muchmore wiped his mouth with his napkin.

"Well, Jeanette," he began, "Bucky was really too young to know she was lonely back then. She was only two. Your mom and I were the ones who knew we wanted a bigger family. When we found out we couldn't have babies of our own after Bucky, we started looking for you and then Harry."

"We always wanted three kids," their mother said. "We have a lot of love to give out — plenty for everybody."

Bucky swallowed a mouthful of roll. "But — " she said, and swallowed again, "doesn't that go for Sparky, too? Isn't there enough love to go around for her?"

Their parents looked at each other for a moment. Mr. Muchmore sat back in his chair and thought.

Bucky watched him.

Jeanette put down her fork and leaned forward.

Harry propped his chin in his hands and bit his lip.

"Sparky," Mr. Muchmore said finally, "really found *us* — " He held up his hand as Bucky began to protest. "Sparky found us, in a way. We didn't go looking for Sparky, now did we? We *did* go looking for Jeanette and Harrison to complete our family. And now we are complete." He smiled at his wife. "What we had to think about — and what you kids have to remember when you think about this family — is what's good for all of us, and how much we can handle."

"And we've thought about Sparky, kids," their mother said. "We think we just can't handle having any more pets."

"We don't mind a few. We *have* a few!" Mr. Muchmore gestured toward two cats. "But if we kept every animal you find, guys, we'd go broke and crazy! Now for exactly a month, we've had only one dog and three cats and I must say, life's been easier."

As the three children continued to stare at him, he took a deep breath and went on. "It's not as if we're not concerned with Sparky's welfare," he said. "We're not going to throw her out in the street, of course."

"Of course!" Jeanette cried, hopeful again.

"But what we are going to do is call Mr. Chesterfield—"

Harry gasped.

"Oh, no—" Bucky began.

"Since he runs the animal shelter, I think he'd be the best person to take charge of Sparky," Mr. Muchmore finished.

"We can't keep Sparky?" Harry asked in a small voice.

"We can't keep Sparky," his father said firmly.

3...

Bucky lay on her top bunk, her head resting on her arms, her sheets kicked into a ball at her feet. She stared at the tiny fluorescent stars Jeanette had glued to their ceiling.

She rolled onto her stomach.

She lurched over again onto her back.

She flipped her pillow so that it would be cooler against her skin.

She sighed loudly.

Below her, Jeanette slept soundly. Bucky's mattress shiftings and bulges did not disturb her dreams. They were filled with fat little puppies toddling on velvety paws.

Bucky lunged over the side and tried to peer into her sister's face, but it was too dark. She didn't see the tiny smile that turned up the corners of Jeanette's mouth. Bucky pulled herself back up on her bed.

There has to be a way, she thought, digging her toes into her wrinkled sheet. There *has* to be a way for Sparky to stay here. If Daddy sends her to the shelter he'll probably never forgive himself. Mom, too. There must be something . . .

"Mmmmmmm," Jeanette murmured in her sleep.

"Jeanette, you up?" Bucky whispered.

Jeanette was silent again.

"Jean*ette*! You *up*?" The whisper was louder this time.

But Jeanette wouldn't leave her dreams.

"I have to think of something," Bucky said aloud, rolling over again. What could I do to make Sparky stay? What could Jeanette do? What could *Harry* do? What could all three of us do together to change Daddy's mind?

Bucky closed her eyes. Nothing, she knew. They had done everything they could have done, said everything they could have said. There was nothing.

Wait a minute! she thought. There is something *Sparky* can do!

Bucky sat bolt upright, kicking her sheets off the end of the bed.

Sparky can have her puppies *tonight*, that's what

16

she can do! If Sparky has puppies tonight, they'll just have to keep her. At least for a while. A long while!

They'll have to.

Bucky hoisted herself over the side of the bed and dropped with a thud to the floor. In Jeanette's dream a puppy tripped over a slipper, and she whimpered slightly.

Bucky didn't hear her. Bucky was tiptoeing out of their room in the dark.

She passed Harry's open door. A shaft of moonlight showed him on his bed facing her, curled in a ball around his Snoopy doll.

Bucky held tight to the banister as she crept down the stairs, but by the time she reached the bottom, her eyes had become more accustomed to the darkness. She could almost hear her heart beating as she made her way through the kitchen to the basement door. At the top of the stairs, she turned on the light, knowing no one would be disturbed except Sparky. And that would be all right.

Ruby looked up from her place on top of the dryer. She liked to sleep there. It was the coolest place in the house for her. Opal preferred a windowsill.

"Hi, Ruby," Bucky whispered, but she barely gave the cat a glance. She knelt beside Sparky, frowning.

"Hey, Spark!" she said. "Where are they?"

Sparky opened one eye. She didn't move.

"Come on, Sparky . . ." Bucky pleaded. "You've *got* to have your little babies tonight!" She pursed her lips, leaned forward and stared intently at the dog's belly.

Gingerly, she reached out one finger and touched a tiny bulge. It moved and she quickly drew her finger back with a small gasp.

"Sparky, *please!*" she whispered into the dog's ear. "*Push* or something!" Sparky snorted and closed her eye. Bucky squinted, made two fists of her hands, leaned forward and grunted loudly.

"Like *that*, Spark," she said. "Do *that*."

Ruby jumped off the dryer and rubbed against Bucky's cotton nightshirt.

"Ruby, how do you make someone have puppies?" Bucky asked, tickling the cat's ear. Ruby turned up her nose and stalked away.

"Okay, Sparky," Bucky said, standing up. "Maybe you don't want to have them in front of me. That's okay." She headed back toward the stairs. "But have them when I'm gone. Please?" With a sigh, she went softly back up to her room.

· · ·

"Jeanette! We overslept! We overslept!"

The sun was streaming in through their bedroom window. Bucky swung her feet over the side of her top bunk.

"Overslept?" Jeanette mumbled drowsily, propping herself up on her elbows. "There's no school, Bucky . . ."

"No, no! The puppies! Sparky may have had her puppies!"

"You think so?" Jeanette asked, awake now.

"If she did, Daddy'll have to let her stay!"

"Come on!" Jeanette cried. "Let's get Harry and go see!"

. . .

In the kitchen, Mrs. Muchmore was setting the children's places. She heard the commotion as they almost fell over each other, tumbling down the stairs. She looked up as they rushed headlong past her toward the basement door, and arrived at the same time. Bucky threw open the door. Harry tried to crawl between the girls' legs.

"Kids," Mrs. Muchmore said calmly, as she put three small glasses on the table, "why don't you all go and wash up?" She poured orange juice into the glasses.

"I want to see —"

"I want to see —"

"*I* want to see —"

"There aren't any puppies yet."

The children slumped.

"Sparky's asleep. Leave her alone now and get ready for breakfast."

"Did Daddy call Mr. Chesterfield?" Jeanette asked.

"No, we thought we'd wait until the sun came up."

"But he *is* going to call," Bucky sighed.

"We discussed that, Bucky," her mother said. "And as a matter of fact, *I'm* going to call. Now how about washing up?"

Slowly, the children moved away from the basement door.

"You sure there aren't any puppies?" Bucky asked.

"It'll be a while yet. Maybe a few days."

"Awwwww," Bucky groaned. "A few days . . . We'll never see them. Sparky'll be packed off to the shelter by that time."

"Maybe we can visit her," Jeanette said without much enthusiasm.

"Well, now," Mrs. Muchmore said, "Sparky is still *here*. And you brought her. So she's still your responsibility. Wash, get dressed and take her for a walk."

"Can you walk a dog while she's pregnant?" Jeanette asked.

Their mother laughed. "Not only *can* you walk her, you'd *better* walk her!"

"Okay," Bucky said, "we'll take her out." The three of them headed dejectedly back toward the stairs.

"And, Jeanette —" Mrs. Muchmore called to her.
"What?"

"During pregnancy you can also cook, clean, shop, swim, work and play tennis!"

"Sparky can do all that?" Harrison asked, wide-eyed, as Bucky dragged him up the stairs.

. . .

Mrs. Muchmore was on the phone when they returned to the kitchen washed and dressed. Bucky's hair wasn't combed.

"Yes, Mr. Chesterfield," they heard their mother say as they slid glumly into their chairs.

"I'm not hungry," Bucky murmured.

"Me neither."

"Me neither."

"*What?*" Mrs. Muchmore said loudly. The children looked up. "But that's terrible!"

"What's terrible?" Jeanette whispered.

"How should I know?" Bucky whispered back.

"Oh, *no!*" Mrs. Muchmore said.

"'Oh, no' *what?*" Harry asked.

"How should *I* know?" Bucky answered.

"I'm so sorry, Mr. Chesterfield," Mrs. Muchmore continued. "I wish we'd had some idea . . . Maybe the town could have helped in some way . . . Yes, I see . . ."

The children leaned toward her from their chairs.

"Well . . . goodbye, Mr. Chesterfield." Mrs. Muchmore hung up. She looked at the three expectant faces.

"The shelter's closing," Mrs. Muchmore said.

"What?"

"What?"

"Huh?"

"Mr. Chesterfield can't take Sparky. The shelter's closing. He can't afford to keep it open. He said their funds have been cut and cut until there's nothing left. He can't take care of the animals he's got, so he's not about to take in any more. Especially a pregnant one . . ."

"Mr. Chesterfield won't take Sparky?" Harry said. His cheeks were bright pink.

"No."

It took almost fifteen seconds for the news to sink in. Then all three Muchmore children burst into whoops and yells. Under the kitchen table, Calpurnia jumped, startled out of her doze. Bucky grabbed Jeanette's arm and began to dance her around the kitchen. Mrs. Muchmore rolled her eyes at the ceiling.

"Yay!" Bucky cried. "Yay yay yay!"

"She still needs a walk," Mrs. Muchmore said, handing them each a different colored vitamin pill. "So please eat your breakfast quickly and get going."

"I will!" Bucky cried. "I'm *starving*!"

"Me, too!" Jeanette cried happily as she spooned up her cereal.

When they finished, Harry raced for the hook near the basement door where they'd kept dog leashes over the years.

"The red one!" he cried. "Let's use the red one for Sparky!" He stood on tiptoe and took it down.

Mrs. Muchmore picked up the kitchen phone again and began to dial. She heard the children clumping happily downstairs at the same time her husband said, "Muchmore here," at the other end of the line.

"Howard?" she said, doodling something that looked like a house on the pad near the phone. "Howard, you're not going to believe this . . ."

4...

Sparky waddled from side to side as the children walked her — slowly — down their street.

"Did you see that?" Jeanette asked. "That little poke in her side? That was one of the puppies!"

"Where?" Harry asked. "Where?"

"Just keep watching her stomach. You'll see."

Harry crouched over as he walked and stared, frowning, at Sparky's belly.

"I think the bath really made her prettier, don't you?" Jeanette asked Bucky, who was holding the leash.

Bucky said, "Well . . ."

"She trusts us. I can tell," Jeanette said. "She knows we're taking care of her."

"How many puppies do you think she'll have?" Harry asked, still hunched over, staring at the dog as he walked.

"I don't know . . . Let's guess," Jeanette said. "We'll take a pool!"

"A poll," Bucky said.

"No, a pool. Like Daddy does for football games."

"Oh! A puppy pool!"

"Right! We'll each take a guess and the one who comes the closest wins."

"Wins what?" Harry asked.

"The pool!" Jeanette cried.

"A swimming pool?" Harry asked.

"No, a money pool," Jeanette told him.

Bucky said, "See—you make a bet. Like a quarter. And we put all the money together and the one who wins gets all of it."

"All the money?" Harry asked and the girls nodded. "I have a quarter," he said.

"Good. Now you have to guess."

"Guess how many puppies?"

"Right."

"Okay . . ." Harry bit his upper lip. "I guess . . . twenty!"

"Fine," Bucky said. "If Sparky has twenty puppies, you win."

"Come on, Bucky," Jeanette said, making a face. "That's not fair. He's only six. Harry, nobody ever had twenty puppies."

"How do you know? Maybe in the *Guinness Book*—" Bucky said.

"Make another guess, Harry," Jeanette said. "She won't have twenty. You'd lose."

Harry frowned. "Fifteen," he said finally.

Bucky looked at her sister. "Still too many, Harry," she conceded. "Guess again."

"But look at her. Look how big! And puppies are so-o little!"

"Less, Harry." Bucky tapped her foot.

"Okay . . . twelve," Harry decided.

Bucky sighed. "I doubt it, but okay. Twelve is your number. I say seven. What about you, Jeanette?"

Jeanette shrugged. "Nine, I guess."

"All right," Bucky said, and poked her brother, sister and herself as she ticked off their bets. "Twelve, nine, seven. Oh, great, there's Bernard! Hey, Bernard!"

Bernard and Rhoda Fishbein were neighbors. He was nine and in Jeanette's class at school.

"Who's that?" Bernard asked, ambling over. Bernard ambled. He rarely walked, he *never* ran.

"This is Sparky," Jeanette said. "Sparky, say hello to Bernard."

Sparky let her tongue fall out of the side of her mouth, where it hung. She stared at the sidewalk.

"Hey, he's gonna have puppies," Bernard commented.

"*She*, Bernard. *She's* going to have puppies."

"Yeah, I know, I know . . ." Bernard pushed his oversized glasses back up on his nose with a forefinger.

"Bernard, how'd you like to be in our pool?" Bucky asked him. "All you have to do is put in a quarter and guess how many puppies Sparky's going to have."

Bernard jiggled some change in his pocket but didn't answer.

"Come on, Bernard, what do you say? We'll walk around and get some other kids, too. The one who guesses right wins all the quarters."

Bernard got down on all fours and stared at Sparky's stomach. Then he crawled around to her other side and stared some more.

"I said 'twelve,'" Harry piped. "But I still think it's twenty."

Bernard frowned. "Can I touch?" he asked.

"If you're really careful," Jeanette said.

"I don't think touching is fair," Bucky said.

"Well, forget it, then," Bernard said.

"Oh, okay, touch, but no counting heads," Bucky said, immediately sorry she hadn't thought of counting heads herself.

Sparky lay down on the sidewalk and rolled onto one side.

"Boy, that makes it easy," Bucky grumbled. "Hurry up, Bernard. She's hot. We'd better take her home."

Bernard softly placed his fingers on different parts of Sparky's stomach. Then he took off his glasses and put his ear against her fur.

"Nobody said anything about *listening*, Bernard," Bucky said.

"I want to make sure what I'm spending a quarter on," Bernard said and listened some more. Then he stood up. "Okay." He reached into his pocket. "Here's the quarter. Your answer is four. Four puppies. No more, no less."

. . .

The Nelkin Falls Town Pool and the sunbathing area surrounding it were filled to capacity on that steaming afternoon. There was barely room to swim, but the children didn't seem to mind. They were wet and cool and could still bob up and down in the water and play confined games of tag. And Harry managed to lie flat in the kiddy pool even though his playmates bumped and ducked him.

Bucky dove happily underwater to grab her friend Marsha's ankles. As Marsha yelped and pulled away, Bucky got a nose full of water. She swam quickly to the surface, her eyes tearing.

"You okay?" Marsha asked, treading water.

Bucky heaved herself up and sat at the edge of the pool, holding her nose.

"Yeah . . ." she said nasally.

Marsha followed her up. "Bernard says you've

got a pregnant dog," she said, wringing out her long hair over her shoulder. "Can I see it?"

"Sure! We want you to join the pool," Bucky answered and winced. "Oooh, my nose hurts." She coughed.

"We did join the pool," Marsha said.

"Not this one. The puppy pool," Bucky told her and explained.

"Guess how many puppies? Okay! Ummmm . . . Let's see . . ."

Jeanette swam up to them with two girls from her class at school.

"Holly and Renee want to see Sparky," Jeanette said. She grabbed Bucky's hands and floated on her stomach, kicking her legs slightly. "Can they come home with us?"

Bucky shrugged. "Sure," she said. "Mom's picking us up at four. Everybody can ride with us."

"We've got fifty cents more," Jeanette said. "They want to bet on the puppies."

"Great."

"Can I go with you, too?" Marsha asked. "I don't have to be home till five and I was going to walk anyway."

"Oh, yeah, my mom won't mind," Bucky said.

"Do you think she'll have them while we're there?" Holly asked. "I never saw puppies being born before. I never saw *anything* being born before."

Bucky shrugged. "She might. Who knows?"

"Ooooh," Renee breathed.

"We've seen babies being born, haven't we, Bucky?" Jeanette said. She let go of Bucky's hands and stood, the waterline coming just to her shoulders. "We had puppies last year . . . And out at Grandpa's farm we saw new kittens . . ."

"I love baby things," Renee sighed. "What time is it?"

"I don't know . . ."

"I hope it's near four. Maybe she had them while we were playing here. I don't want to miss seeing them."

But the water felt so good and the air so sticky, they lost track of time and Bucky was surprised when she looked up to see her mother gesturing at her.

"Oh! Mom!" she called, spluttering. "Marsha and Renee and Holly are coming with us, okay? Marsha! My mom's here!"

"What — ?" Mrs. Muchmore began, but the five girls were clambering out of the pool.

"They want to see Sparky," Bucky said as she grabbed for a towel.

Mrs. Muchmore noticed that all their towels were already soaked, and with Harry, there'd be six wet youngsters slithering around on her car seats. With a sigh, she reached for Harry's hand and clutched air.

"Now where's Harrison?" she said, looking around. "He was right here . . ."

"Mom!" Harry cried, appearing from behind her. "Bernard's coming with us. And Nicholas! They want to—"

"—see Sparky. I know. I wonder if the car can stand this . . ."

But all eight kids piled in excitedly, crowding together, sitting on laps.

"She didn't have them yet, did she, Mrs. Muchmore?" Renee asked.

"Yeah, we didn't miss anything, did we, Mom?" Jeanette wanted to know.

Her mother squirmed in her seat and pulled out a damp towel. "Nope. You didn't miss anything."

"Bucky said the shelter was closing," Marsha said. She was in the front seat between Mrs. Muchmore and Bucky. "So you get to keep Sparky."

"For a while, Marsha . . . But it's terrible news about the shelter. The number of homeless animals in Nelkin Falls isn't going to get any smaller. Not to mention the animals that are at the shelter now, being taken care of . . ."

"What'll happen to them?" Jeanette piped from the back seat.

"I don't know, honey . . ."

"Mr. Chesterfield will have to find homes for them," Renee said.

"Yeah . . ." Jeanette said, "but what if he can't? What'll happen?"

"He'll keep them himself," Bucky said. "Won't he?"

Mrs. Muchmore attempted a smile.

"How many are there?" Jeanette asked. Her mother shrugged. "Don't you know? Mom?"

"No, honey."

"If Mr. Chesterfield can't keep them," Bernard said, "you know what'll happen."

"What?" Renee asked.

"You know." He said it solemnly.

"No!" Jeanette burst out. She knew what Bernard meant. She remembered when one of their cats had—

"*What?*" Holly cried. "What, Bernard?"

"He'll put them to sleep."

"He won't!" Marsha gasped.

"He'll have to," Bernard said. "It's the most humane way. He can't just turn them loose."

Jeanette put her thumb in her mouth. She did that only when she was very nervous or upset. And she forgot that she never did it in public.

Bucky shifted her feet nervously next to Marsha. "Sparky's puppies will have good homes," she said. "We'll make sure of that . . ."

Mrs. Muchmore pulled into their driveway, and the kids untangled themselves and jumped out of the car.

"Through the basement door!" Mrs. Muchmore cried as they all headed for the front door—and the living room.

Jeanette hung back.

"Mom?" she said as her mother started for the house.

"Mmm?"

Jeanette looked into her mother's face for a moment. "Nothing," she said.

"You okay?" Mrs. Muchmore asked.

Jeanette nodded, holding her hands behind her back. Then she turned, and followed the others into the basement.

. . .

They all sat on the cool cement floor. They had arranged themselves in a small circle around Sparky, and were listening intently as Bucky licked the tip of her pencil and read the totals aloud from her notebook.

"Okay," she said. "I've got myself, seven. Jeanette, nine. Harry, twelve. Bernard, four. Holly, six. Marsha, eight. Right?"

"And me! I've got three!"

"Oh, right." Bucky checked her pad. "Nicholas, three. That's everybody, isn't it?"

"No . . . I haven't picked yet."

"Well, come on, Renee, we haven't got all day. Pick a number."

"Don't rush me, Bucky, I'm thinking."

Bucky tapped her pencil. Renee peered at Sparky, who suddenly snored loudly.

"I guess . . ." Renee said, "two."

"Okay." Bucky wrote it, then mumbled to herself. "Me, Jeanette, mmm, hmm, Holly, mm, mmm, Renee. Eight. So we've got exactly two dollars. Jeanette?"

Jeanette was staring at her lap.

"Hey, Jeanette!"

"What?" she asked, looking up.

"We've got two dollars. In the pool." Jeanette looked blank. "In the puppy pool, Jeanette. Are you in there?" Bucky rapped lightly on Jeanette's forehead and Holly laughed.

"We need more people," Bernard said.

"Well, we can't have any more people," Bucky told him. "How many numbers can there be for puppies, anyway? I mean, she *can't* have any more than seven."

"She can have twelve!" Harry cried.

"Nobody picked one," Bernard said. "Or five."

"We have enough," Bucky said. "And two dollars is a good profit for only spending a quarter. Right, Jeanette?"

Jeanette was frowning.

"What's the matter?" Marsha asked, poking her.

Jeanette suddenly shivered in the damp basement air.

"We have to go down there," she said softly.

"Where?" Marsha asked.

"To the shelter."

"The shelter?"

"What for?" Bernard asked.

"To save them!" Jeanette said, hugging herself. "To save the animals!"

They all looked at her.

"Well, we do . . ." Her lower lip trembled. "They're all nice little puppies and kittens and dogs and cats and they're sweet and not even sick, so how could we let Mr. Chesterfield put them all to sleep? Without even trying!"

"What can *we* do?" Holly asked.

"Yeah . . ." from Nicholas.

"We have to do *something*," Jeanette said and looked at her sister. "Bucky, we have to do *something*! And tomorrow, too! First thing!"

"Like what?"

"Like some of us could go down there and talk to Mr. Chesterfield."

"You mean a committee," Marsha said.

"Yes!" Jeanette cried. "A committee! *We'll* do it — Bucky and Harry and I. The Muchmore Committee!"

5...

Mr. Chesterfield was a small, round man. He had lots of very white hair and a big white mustache that Bucky was sure had to be false. She had never seen another mustache that size. It stood out firm and thick from Mr. Chesterfield's upper lip and curled at the ends like twisted paper.

"Nice of you kids to be concerned," Mr. Chesterfield said. Bucky watched his mustache bob up and down.

"Can we see the animals?" Jeanette asked, and then added, "Please?"

"I'm sorry I couldn't take your doggy," Mr. Chesterfield said. "I guess your mom told you the spot we're in here . . ."

"Don't worry about Sparky," Harry said brightly. "We can take care of her!"

"Could we please see the animals?" Jeanette asked again.

"I've got a cat with four kittens, eight weeks old," Mr. Chesterfield said, pulling at his mustache. "Breaks my heart, it does."

"What we'd like to do is help you find them all homes," Jeanette said.

"Ours!" Harry yelled and Bucky put a hand on his shoulder.

"We formed a committee to work on it. The Muchmore Committee," Jeanette added proudly.

"Well, that's nice. Really nice. Why don't you come on back and you can have a look."

Jeanette was first at the big steel door when Mr. Chesterfield opened it. They all followed him into a room with white walls and a tile floor.

"It smells like Grandma's bathroom," Harry noted, wrinkling his nose.

"It's disinfectant," Mr. Chesterfield said, and Harry said, "Oh," and nodded, though he didn't understand the word.

"Awww, look," Jeanette said, peering into one of the steel cages. "Pussycat . . ." she crooned.

"*ROWR!*" the cat said and Jeanette drew back.

"He's mean, that one," Mr. Chesterfield said. "Don't get near him, sis. I picked him up behind the supermarket while he was scrounging through the garbage. Nearly clawed me to death. Had to sedate him just to get him into the van."

"Kitties can't be mean," Jeanette said and put her hand through the wires of the cage. Bucky grabbed her arm and pulled it back.

"*Don't*, Jeanette!" she said. "Didn't you hear Mr. Chesterfield?"

"But animals trust me," Jeanette insisted. "They *do*, Mr. Chesterfield."

"Sis, it's hard to trust anybody if all you've gotten is kicked all your life." He touched the top of the cat cage. "Now, Awful here, he never had a kind word or a pat in all his days. Now, maybe with a lot of patience and a lot of time and love he'd be okay. Thing is, we don't have a lot of time . . ."

"Awful?" Jeanette said.

Mr. Chesterfield nodded.

Jeanette turned back to the cage. "Oh, Awful, you just need lots of love, that's all you need," she said softly. "I could make you trust people, I know I could . . ."

"*Rrrr-rrr,*" Awful growled, lifting his upper lip into a sneer.

"I want this one, Buck!" Harry called. He had wandered down the corridor, which was filled with cages on both sides. "Look, Bucky! Look, Jeanette! Let's take this one!"

"Aw, Harry . . . Don't make us feel worse," Bucky said. "Mom was not kidding this morning. Sparky is *it*."

"Oh, but just *look* at her," Harry pleaded and stamped his foot for emphasis. "Ple-ease?"

Bucky and Jeanette walked toward Harry, with Mr. Chesterfield trailing behind.

"Ah, that's Winsome," Mr. Chesterfield said.

The dog had a large, shepherd-like head, but with huge, floppy ears that dipped sideways. It stood on pudgy legs and looked completely out of proportion, as if a kindergartner had made it out of leftover pieces of clay.

"Awwwww," Jeanette said, "Look at those eyes . . ."

The eyes were large and round — intelligent eyes that gazed at the Muchmores with hope and excitement and a love of play.

"She's too funny-looking for most folks," Mr. Chesterfield said. "Not what you'd call a 'status dog.'"

"She is too a spatis dog," Harry insisted. "She's the best spatis dog I ever saw!"

"Forget it, Harry," Bucky said in her firmest older-sister voice. She opened her notebook. "Now, this is what I figure . . . We're here to write down how many animals you have, what they are, and — and —"

"And probably you'll want their medical histories," Mr. Chesterfield offered and twirled the end of his mustache.

"Yeah. What shots they've had and stuff."

Mr. Chesterfield nodded. "I appreciate your help, sis," he said. "Okay. I've got the tiger cat you saw back there. His name's Awful. Mean, real mean. But he's got everything—rabies, distemper, hepatitis, Lepto C-1, feline panleukopenia—"

"It's okay," Bucky said, scribbling rapidly, "I'll just say, 'All Shots.'"

"You can say he's been wormed, too. But not neutered yet."

Bucky wrote.

"And there's Sweetie, she's the mama with four kittens I told you about—"

Jeanette was crooning to them, making soft little sounds and stroking them with her fingers.

"I haven't named them yet," Mr. Chesterfield went on. "Breaks my heart, just breaks my heart . . ."

Bucky continued to write while Jeanette and Harry moved around and examined all the animals, cooing and clucking their tongues.

"We're going to find wonderful people for you," Jeanette said, spreading her arms. "*All* of you."

When they were finished, Bucky's tally included eight cats and six dogs. Her hand was aching from all that writing and she was glad to put her pencil and pad back in her pocket, but Mr. Chesterfield stopped her.

"There's one more," he said. "In the back."

"By itself?" Harry asked. "All alone?"

"All alone," Mr. Chesterfield said, nodding. "Come on."

The children looked at each other as they followed him into the back rooms, where he lived and had his private office.

They heard the screeching as soon as he opened the door.

"It's a bird!" Jeanette cried. "A parrot!"

"Nope." Mr. Chesterfield smiled under his mustache.

"A mouse," Harry guessed. "A *big* mouse."

"Nope."

"A screech owl?" Bucky asked.

"Nope."

"What, then? Show us!" Harry peered around the small living room.

"Over there," Mr. Chesterfield said, pointing to his little office. "Near the desk."

Bucky saw it first and gasped.

"It's a monkey!" she cried. "A real live monkey!"

"But it's so tiny!" Jeanette breathed.

"It's a squirrel monkey. She's tiny, but she's managed to keep me up every night since I got her."

Jeanette crept closer to the monkey's large cage. "Does she bite?" she asked.

"No-o. Not her. She cuddles. She *loves* to cuddle." Mr. Chesterfield clicked his tongue. "Some folks bought her for their kids and decided she was too much trouble and too noisy. That happens a lot. You've got to be pretty sure what you're doing when you get yourself a pet. Otherwise . . . some poor animal's just shuffled off . . ."

"*I'll* take her!" Harry said firmly.

Bucky frowned at him.

"What's her name?" Jeanette asked.

"Cuddles," Mr. Chesterfield answered.

"Cuddles! I want her!" Harry said. "Couldn't we take her home, Bucky? Just to *show* Daddy and Mommy? I *know* they'd want her! They would, Mr. Chesterfield. Couldn't I take her home to *show*?"

Mr. Chesterfield shook his head. "Can't let 'em out, son," he said. "None of 'em. Not even for a day. See, son, they've been flea-dipped and disinfected . . . If I let 'em out, they'd be exposed to all kinds of things and then I couldn't guarantee to folks that they were completely healthy."

Harry stuck out his lower lip.

"Sorry, son," Mr. Chesterfield said kindly. "You have to be a grown-up to take an animal, and you have to be able to keep her."

Bucky exhaled. "Cuddles," she said, almost to herself, and cataloged the monkey.

Jeanette looked around the small quarters.

"When they close the shelter . . ." she began, "will you have to move, Mr. Chesterfield?"

He pulled in his lips until all she saw was mustache.

"Mmm-ph," he mumbled. "Well." He cleared his throat. "What we've got to do is find homes for *them*, first" — he nodded toward the long room filled with cages — "and then me. And then . . . me."

"You had all your shots?" Harrison asked.

6...

"We need Mom's address wheel," Bucky said, as the three of them raced for the front door. "You get it, Jeanette, and I'll—"

"What is it?" Jeanette asked. She was right behind her sister.

"Door's locked. Mom must be out."

"I'll get the key!" Harry cried and ran around to the back, where the extra was kept inside Calpurnia's doghouse.

They found Mrs. Muchmore's note on the kitchen table. Jeanette read it out loud. "'Dear Kids: I'm out on a demonstration. There's lunch in the fridge—tuna fish for Bucky, yogurt for Jeanette, PB and J for Harry. (Harry, don't smear the peanut butter.) It's okay for you to walk to the pool and I'll pick you up there later. Love, Mom.' Will we have time to go to the pool?"

"I doubt it," Bucky said. "We may be on the phone all afternoon."

"I want my peanut butter and jelly," Harry said, heading for the refrigerator.

"Wait, Harry. First get a big pad and some pencils. And sharpen 'em. Jeanette, you get the address wheel. I'll meet you upstairs."

"Can I bring my yogurt?"

"Yeah. And bring my tuna fish. And milk."

"I can't carry all that, Bucky!"

"Okay, okay . . . I'll bring the food."

Bucky was sitting on her mother's bed when they ran in with the things she wanted.

"Good," Bucky said, taking the address wheel from Jeanette. "Here, Jeanette. You take this pad and pencil and write what I tell you." Bucky twisted the address wheel and the small cards with the names, addresses and phone numbers of Mrs. Muchmore's customers flopped forward. She stopped at a name she recognized, picked up the telephone, and dialed.

"Hello, Mrs. Shiminsky? This is Bucky Muchmore, your neighbor. Fine, thank you, how are you? They're fine, too. How is your family? Okay, Mrs. Shiminsky, the reason I'm calling is, I haven't seen any pets around your house and I was thinking that maybe you need—what? Oh, she is? She does? Cats *and* dogs, too? How about monkeys? Oh. Okay. Thanks, anyway . . ." Bucky hung up.

"What happened?" Jeanette asked.

"Her little girl is allergic to fur. She breaks out in red blotches all over her body if she gets near anything with fur."

"Oh, that's *awful*," Jeanette cried. "Imagine not being able to hold a puppy . . ."

"Yeah . . ." Harry said. They all looked at the floor for a moment in sympathy for little Mary Shiminsky. Then Bucky picked up the address wheel and the phone again.

"Hello, Mr. Spartanburg? This is Bucky Muchmore. We buy all our shoes at your shop. Yes, I know my mother sold you your blinds . . . She wants to know how you like them. Two years ago? Oh. Well, we were wondering, Mr. Spartanburg, if you needed a watchdog around your place. A *watch*dog. In case you're held up or anything. No, no, I haven't heard of any robberies lately, it's just that it's good to be prepared, right? Oh . . . Well, then, how about—just a pet? You do? Okay . . . thanks, anyway . . ." She hung up.

"What'd he say?" Jeanette asked.

"He has a Saint Bernard. It eats him out of house and home. He wants to get rid of it."

"Listen, Bucky, what am I supposed to be writing, anyway?"

"All the names of the interested people."

"Oh."

Bucky pulled "Spartanburg" and "Shiminsky" out of the address wheel. "Here," she said, handing the small cards to Jeanette. "It'll be easier if we just take out the cards. That way we'll know who we called. I'll finish the *S*'s first. *S* was always a good letter for me. Besides, there are a lot of them in here."

Bucky went through the *S*'s. Then she called all the *P*'s. Then the *M*'s. After an hour, Jeanette and Harry were each holding a stack of small cards.

"This isn't any good," Bucky said. "We're not getting anywhere."

"I can see that," Jeanette said, shuffling her cards.

"We need to get the animals out of the shelter," Bucky said, tapping one finger against her cheek.

"Yay!" Harry cried. "Let's take them out! Let's bring them home!"

"No, Harry, no," Bucky said. "I don't mean for us to bring them home. We can't, anyway. A grown-up has to take an animal from the shelter. Kids can't do it."

"And we can't borrow them either," Jeanette said. "Mr. Chesterfield said that."

"But we need to get them, because if we show them to people, then they won't be able to say no. Just like Harry."

"Just like us," Jeanette added.

"Yeah. Just like us."

"Well, how do we do that?" Jeanette asked. "How do we get the animals out of the shelter to take them around?"

Bucky tapped her finger faster, nervously, and didn't answer.

"Are you thinking, Bucky?" Harry asked.

"Yeah, I'm thinking," she answered.

She was thinking so hard, she didn't hear the front door open and close.

"Mom's home," Harry said.

"What?"

"I said Mom's home."

"*I'm home!*" came a call from downstairs. "Kids? Bucky?"

"We're up here!" Jeanette left the bedroom and met her mother halfway up the stairs.

"Why didn't you go to the pool?" Mrs. Muchmore asked. "It was so hot! What are you doing home?"

"We're working. We've been trying to find homes for the shelter animals. We're the Muchmore Committee."

"I see . . ."

"We called people up on the phone," Harry said

from the head of the stairs. "We told them all about the animals and asked them if they wanted one."

Mrs. Muchmore smiled. "That was nice, Harry. Well, come on . . . Let's go back downstairs. I've got some things to put away . . ."

Jeanette and Harry followed her into the kitchen.

"Harrison," Mrs. Muchmore said, "did you get my note?"

"Uh-huh."

"What did it say?"

"It said that lunch was in the refrigerator and we could go to the pool . . ."

"What else?"

"'Love, Mom?'"

"Besides that."

"'Don't smear the peanut butter.'"

"Right. Wipe it off the refrigerator door, please." He did and she mussed his hair. "Did you have any luck with your phone calls?"

"No . . ." Jeanette shook her head. "Not yet. But we'll find people. I know we will. Bucky's up there in the bedroom thinking right now."

. . .

Bucky was still thinking when their parents called them to dinner that evening. She was thinking so hard she scowled.

"Bucky, what's wrong?" her father asked.

"Wrong? Nothing!"

"The way you were staring at your macaroni I thought you were going to bite the plate."

Bucky relaxed the muscles in her face. "No, Dad . . . I'm just trying to figure out a way to make people want to—"

The phone rang. Bucky jumped.

"That might be someone calling back to say they want a kitty or a dog after all! I'll get it!"

"Now, Bucky, you finish your dinner. I'll get it." Mrs. Muchmore reached over and took the receiver from its cradle on the wall.

"Hello?" she said. "Oh, hello, Bernard. How are you? And Rhoda? And your parents? That's good. Bucky? Well, may she call you back, Bernard? She's having—"

"I'm finished!" Bucky said, her mouth full. She swallowed hard. "I'm done." Her mother passed her the receiver with a shake of her head. "Hi, Bernard!"

"Hi, Bucky. Anything new?"

"Well . . ." she began, "there are eight cats and six dogs . . ."

"No, I mean anything new with *Sparky*," Bernard said. "Did she have them yet?"

"The puppies? No, she didn't have them yet . . . But we have to start getting homes for the shelter animals, Bernard. Boy, he has some really nice ones there . . . People would love them. Wouldn't you like a nice cat, Bernard?"

"Cats eat hamsters."

"They do not."

"Tell that to my mother. Anyway, I can't take anything now. We have a houseguest. And he's got a duck."

"Who?" Bucky asked. "Is it a kid?"

"Almost. It's my uncle. He's a magician."

"A real magician?"

"Yup. He did his act for Rhoda and me today. I would have called but I knew you were at the shelter."

"Mostly I was on the phone, Bernard."

Harry leaned over toward Bucky. "Who's a magician?" he asked.

"Just a minute, Bernard." Bucky put her hand over the mouthpiece. "Bernard's uncle is visiting him. He's a magician. He did his act for Bernard and Rhoda while we were at the shelter."

"Would he do it for us?" Harry asked. "I want to see a real magician!"

Bucky turned back to the phone. "Hey, Bernard?" she said. "Would your uncle do his act for us if we came over?"

"I don't know . . . I'll ask him. Hold on. *Hey, Uncle Lenny!*"

Bucky winced and pulled the phone away from her ear as Bernard yelled. "He's asking, Harry," she told her brother.

Bernard came back to the phone. "He says sure.

He needs the practice. See, he's on his way to Las Vegas to be a headliner."

"A what?"

"A headliner. That's what he says. A star. He figures he'll start as a warm-up act in the lounge of a big hotel."

"Wow," Bucky said.

"What?" Harry asked.

"He's going to be a big star in Las Vegas," Bucky whispered.

Mr. and Mrs. Muchmore exchanged looks.

"Bernard," Bucky said into the phone, "we're coming over."

"Great! Maybe I'll call some other kids, too," Bernard said.

"You have to walk Sparky before you go anywhere," Mrs. Muchmore said.

Bucky nodded. "We have to walk Sparky," she told Bernard, "and then we'll be over. I hope he's good, Bernard . . ."

"He's very good. He always wanted to be a magician. He was in podiatry school until June. Then he dropped out to do magic full time instead of just on weekends at the Elks Club."

"See you later, Bernard," Bucky said and hung up.

"A magic show, eh?" Mr. Muchmore said. "That should be fun."

"Maybe he's a good enough magician to make wishes come true," Jeanette said with a sigh.

"Now, I'm sure those animals will be fine," Mrs. Muchmore said. "Take care of Sparky and go over and enjoy the show."

7...

Bernard's living room was filled with children when the Muchmores arrived. His uncle was nowhere in sight.

"Hi, Bucky!"

"Oh, hi, Marsha!" Bucky looked around. She spotted Nicholas and Holly and a bunch of younger children Bernard had rounded up for the show.

"Is he really good, Bernard?" Jeanette asked. "Will he make a tiger disappear?"

"A tiger? In my living room? Are you kidding?"

"What's he doing here, anyway, Bernard?" Bucky asked. "And where is he?"

"He's going to make an entrance. My sister's going to introduce him," Bernard said. "And he's here to visit us for a few days. Mostly so my father will tune up his car for the trip."

"Is that his RV in the driveway?"

"Yeah," Bernard said, nodding. "It's brand-new used. You should see the inside. He made a separate room in the back for all his stuff. He's got costumes . . . and a saw . . . and scarves and big hats and colored boxes and a magic wand . . ."

"A magic wand?" Harry's eyes were wide.

"Sure, every magician needs a magic wand," Jeanette said.

"His is plastic," Bernard said.

"When's he coming out, Bernard?" Holly called from her seat on the floor.

"Yeah, when?" Harry asked.

"Soon. He's getting dressed. He's got a neat cape. It's got purple shiny stuff inside."

Just then, Bernard's sister Rhoda tapped a spoon against a glass. The living room became silent.

"Ladies — and — Gentlemen!" Rhoda screeched. "Now appearing for the first time in Nelkin Falls — the magic of — *The Great Leonardo!*"

"My Uncle Lenny," Bernard whispered proudly.

The kids sitting on the chairs, couch and floor, applauded and cheered.

Rhoda moved toward a small table, which held an ashtray, a vase and a small lighted lamp. She picked up the lamp and moved its shade, focusing it on the kitchen door.

The door swung open and a tall man with a pointed beard, long black cape and black top-hat swept into the room, shielding his eyes from the glare of the lamp.

"Hello, hello, hello!" The Great Leonardo sang at the crowd, and then murmured under his breath, "Hold the lamp down, Rhoda."

"Hello!" the kids sang back.

"Hello, Uncle Lenny!" Bernard yelled.

"How many of you out there believe in magic?" Leonardo called.

"I do, I do!" Harry cried, jumping up and down.

"A very smart young man!" Leonardo observed. "I want that very smart young man right up here at the front with me!"

Harry rushed up, stepping on and over kids on the way.

"Look, willya, he picked Harry," Jeanette said, smiling.

"He wouldn't pick me," Bernard said, "because I'm a relative."

Rhoda focused the lamp on Harry, who didn't seem to mind.

"What's your name, son?" Leonardo asked in a loud voice.

"Harry . . . Harrison Watt Muchmore," Harry said, grinning.

"Well! A most impressive name!" Leonardo pro-nounced. "And what is a young man with such an impressive name doing *with*" — he reached toward the neck of Harry's shirt — "*a banana* behind his ear!" He held up the banana as Rhoda crashed two toy cymbals together and the kids cheered. Harry blushed.

"*And*," Leonardo continued, "A *carrot* in his belt!" He pulled a gigantic fake carrot from Harry's side. The kids cheered again. Rhoda clashed the cymbals.

"*Thank* you, Harrison Watt Muchmore!" Leonardo boomed and a smiling Harry stepped back over the audience toward his sisters.

"And now — my world-famous *cape trick*!"

Leonardo continued his act, whirling his cape and pulling out scarves, balloons and streamers, which he threw over the heads of his audience. The children grabbed for them, knocking over the table with the vase and the ashtray on it. Mrs. Fishbein rushed over with a dustpan, a broom and a pained expression, but Leonardo ignored it all and went on with his act. He sawed Holly in half, which wasn't easy because she giggled the entire time, and he pulled coins out of the ears of Nicholas and a tot named Kippy.

"Doug Henning is better," Bucky whispered to Jeanette.

"*Yay!*" the kids screamed as Leonardo held up a big green bottle with flowers sticking out of the top and made it disappear.

"And for my last trick —" he thundered at them,

as he whirled his big top-hat around and around. *ABRACADABRA, METAMORPHOSIS, ZINGER, SINGER, ZAP!*" He reached inside the hat and pulled out a bewildered-looking white duck.

"Ahhhhhhh!" the children breathed.

"Hey, that was pretty good!" Bucky said and clapped her hands.

"Thank you, thank you very much!" Leonardo said and bowed. Then, he swept back through the kitchen door while Rhoda was deciding whether to crash her cymbals or focus the lamp.

The kids yawned and stretched. Some of their parents had arrived to pick them up and they began to trudge out the door with their streamers and balloons.

"That was fun," Marsha said as she passed the Muchmores. Then she yawned. "How was it at the shelter today?" she asked.

"Oh. You reminded me. Now I feel bad again," Jeanette said. She had been happily toying with a balloon twisted into the shape of a dachshund.

"We have to find a way to get the animals out of the shelter so we can show them to people," Bucky told Marsha. "And Mr. Chesterfield won't let us borrow them. We're out of ideas. We don't know what to do."

"Oh . . ." Marsha said, frowning. "Well, if you think of anything, let me know . . ."

"Yeah, we will."

"'Night, Bernard. Thanks!"

"'Night, Marsha . . ."

Mr. and Mrs. Fishbein had gone to the front door, where they were saying good night to everyone and kicking confetti off their stoop.

"He's great, isn't he?" Bernard said to Bucky.

"I liked the duck," Bucky said.

"How did he do that?" Harry asked.

"It's magic, Harry," Bernard answered.

"Can we meet him? Your uncle?" Jeanette asked.

"Sure. But wait till he changes. Come on, you missed the punch and pretzels." He led them over to the sideboard, where some snacks were still left.

"He's great," Bernard repeated. "I'm sure he'll get a job."

"I thought you said he had a job," Bucky said.

"No, he *wants* a job," Bernard told her. "Out in Vegas—"

"—as a warm-up act in the lounge of a hotel. I know," Bucky said.

"I don't know where that banana came from," Harry said.

"Where's the duck?" Jeanette asked. "What did he do with the duck?"

There was a scream from the kitchen.

Bucky was at the door first.

"It's okay," Rhoda said. "The duck scared me. It poked its beak into the back of my leg."

The duck was wandering around the kitchen,

quacking, as the bearded man came in wearing jeans and looking a lot younger in his Durrell School of Podiatry T-shirt.

"Hi," he said. "Hi, there, Harrison."

"Are you The Great Leonardo?" Harry asked. He wasn't sure, without the cape and hat.

"Yep. But right now, I'm Lenny Graber, ex-almost foot doctor and future star." He leaned down and petted the duck absently. "How'd you like the act?"

"Great!" Harry said.

"Pretty good," Jeanette said.

Bucky shrugged.

"What's wrong?" Lenny asked, frowning. "Everything went off without a hitch."

"Well, yeah, but all that stuff's been done," Bucky said. "The sawing the girl in half, the scarves, the pulling stuff out of a hat—"

"Hey, listen, kid, if you think it's easy yankin' a *duck* out of—"

"You asked," Bucky said with another shrug.

"This is a terrific act!" Lenny said, frowning at Bucky. "I'll be a Vegas headliner before you hit junior high!"

"Yeah," Bernard said, glaring at Bucky. "He's a great magician!"

The great magician playfully grabbed the back of Bernard's neck. "He's my biggest fan," he said with a smile.

"Well, it was nice of you to do the show for us," Jeanette said. "I mean . . . it was free and all . . ."

"That's right," Lenny said. "Soon, people will be putting down big bucks to catch my act."

"I dunno . . ." Bucky said.

Lenny put both his hands on his hips. "What's with you, anyway, kid? Can't you appreciate a class act when you see one? Do you know how long I've been working on this? What you were privileged to witness tonight took *years*. Man, the time I spent in front of the mirror, down in the basement, out in the woods, at my mother's tea parties—"

"I liked the duck," Bucky said, interrupting. She had her idea. "I think you need more animals for your act."

"Huh?"

"I think animals would be good. Everyone loves animals. You could do more tricks with them. Then you'd have something!"

"Did you say animals?"

"Yeah. Animals. Dogs. Cats. A monkey. Definitely a monkey!"

"A monkey?"

Jeanette looked at Bucky wide-eyed. Harry sat down on the floor and put the duck on his lap.

"See?" Bucky said, nodding at Harry. "Kids especially love animals."

"A monkey?" Lenny repeated.

61

"We could get you one," Bucky said. "Probably —
like *that!*" She snapped her fingers.

Lenny caught his lower lip between his teeth. "A
monkey . . ." he muttered.

"Would you excuse me for a minute?" Bucky
said politely. "I'd like to talk to my sister in the
other room."

"May I come?" Bernard asked.

"Sure," Bucky said. "It's *your* uncle."

The three of them walked back into the living
room, leaving the magician drinking coffee, Rhoda
doing dishes and Harry petting the duck.

"What is it?" Jeanette asked.

"Don't you get it?" Bucky said. She looked at
Bernard. "Your uncle needs a better act. Animals
would make it better. Wouldn't they?"

Bernard looked blank.

"Well, wouldn't they?"

"Maybe . . ." Bernard said. "It'd probably
make his act a little different from other magic acts
. . . A bunch of animals . . . A *monkey?*"

"Mr. Chesterfield has a monkey. It's adorable.
Your uncle would love it. The duck would love it.
And there are cute dogs and cats . . . And that
would be the answer to everything! The animals
get a good home with your uncle and your uncle
gets a better act. Well?"

"Gee, Bucky, that's a terrific idea!" Jeanette
cried, and clapped her hands together.

"Yeah . . . maybe," Bernard said.

"Well, why don't we go in and ask him?" Bucky said.

"Let's!" Jeanette said eagerly.

They went back into the kitchen. Bucky opened her mouth, but Lenny began to talk. He wasn't looking at the kids—he was staring straight ahead, scratching his ear. His voice sounded dreamy.

"I could put a monkey in my silver hat. No. The blue one. No. The fedora with the stars on it. Yeah! And the monkey could wear a little vest with the same stars—to match! Hey! Yeah! And a dog—if I had a couple of dogs—I could do that illusion with the transference from under the table to the inside of the box—"

"I can get you a couple of dogs!" Bucky shrieked.

"Sh!" Lenny said. He was still staring into space. "And the illusion would be even better if one dog was big and one was little . . ."

Bucky grinned and poked Jeanette, who was too excited to do anything but dance in place on her toes.

"Oh! And a cat! I once read about this trick, where a cat appears to be sleeping in *midair* . . . Now, how was that done again . . . ?"

"So it's a deal?" Bucky said.

"Huh?"

"It's a deal, I said. We get you the animals. You get a new act."

"I like the idea . . ." Lenny said thoughtfully.

Then: "Where can you kids get animals like that?"

"*Well*," Bucky said, rubbing her hands together, "it just so happens that we know of an animal shelter that's going out of business and needs to find homes for the animals it has left."

"Oh, yeah . . .?"

"Yeah. And there are dogs and cats—big and little—and a monkey and everything! And you're an adult, so you could take them!"

"He's not a real adult," Bernard said. "He was just in school."

"But he's over eighteen," Bucky said. "That counts as an adult."

"I know . . . But I don't like to think of Uncle Lenny as an 'a-dult.' You know . . ."

"Think of him as a scrambled egg, Bernard!" Bucky cried. "The whole point is, everyone gets to be happy."

Lenny was nodding his head. It just might beef up the act. It just might. I've seen magicians and I've seen animals . . ."

"Everyone *loves* animals!" Jeanette cried. She bent down to pet the duck on Harry's lap.

Harry grinned up at her. "His name's Chuck," he said, smoothing wing feathers. "Chuck Duck. Isn't that a good name?"

8...

"How was the magician?" Mrs. Muchmore asked when the kids came home.

"Terrific!" Harry said.

"Better than terrific," Jeanette said. "He's going to give all the shelter animals a home!"

"He's what?" Mr. Muchmore asked.

"He's going to take them all and put them in his act!" Bucky said.

"No kidding?"

"No kidding! Isn't that great?"

"I told you everything would work out," Mrs. Muchmore said.

"Bucky, are you sure about this?" her father asked. "That's an awfully big responsibility . . ."

"He knows! He's got ideas already! You should

have heard him making up new stuff for them to do!"

"And he's nice," Jeanette said. "The animals will be happy with him. And he'll be happy and all the people who watch them will be happy. Boy, am I happy!"

"Well, I'm happy everyone's happy," Mr. Muchmore said. "I walked Sparky, by the way . . ."

The dog had moved up from the basement. She and Calpurnia lay panting — at some distance from each other — on the kitchen linoleum.

"Thanks, Daddy," Jeanette said and knelt to pet her. "How is she?"

"All right," Mrs. Muchmore answered, "for being barefoot and pregnant in the middle of July in Nelkin Falls. I'm not sure how much longer she's got. Dad said she took one step, then stopped to breathe — another step — then another breath. Maybe it's just the heat."

"Sounds like Mrs. Mahaffy from down the block," Bucky observed and her father laughed.

"Well, Sparky's all right, though. She may seem listless and droopy, but she eats like a horse," Mrs. Muchmore said.

"Just like Mrs. Mahaffy!" Mr. Muchmore said.

"Why don't you all go up to bed now?" Mrs. Muchmore suggested.

"Yeah, we'd better," Bucky said. "We have a big day tomorrow."

"You do?"

"Well, yeah! We're going down to the shelter with Bernard's uncle!"

Jeanette was nodding. "He said we could be there when he takes them all out. We can help him get them back to Bernard's and we'll be able to hold them and everything . . ."

"Are you *really* sure about all this?" Mr. Muchmore repeated.

"Yes, Dad!" Bucky insisted. "We're sure!"

"Bucky, maybe we should call the other kids, too," Jeanette suggested. "Marsha and Renee and Holly and Nicholas . . . They'd want to see all the animals . . . And they could help, too! Bernard's uncle will need us for a while to help get the animals calm and settled and all . . ."

Bucky nodded. "Good idea," she said.

Mr. Muchmore leaned against the kitchen wall. "Does he have an assistant?" he asked.

"Who?"

"Bernard's uncle."

"Uh . . . no . . . Just Rhoda. Why?"

Mr. Muchmore sighed. "I just can't imagine how he can handle all those animals, that's all."

"Oh, Daddy!" Jeanette said and patted his arm. "It'll be no trouble at all!"

. . .

Bucky sat down in her mother's bedroom chair

and picked up the notebook she had left next to the phone. Sparky lay between her feet.

"I'm looking at what we're getting," she said as Jeanette came in. "'Sweetie,'" she read aloud. "'Two-year-old black-and-tan female cat . . .' what's this word?"

Jeanette leaned over her shoulder. "'Loving,'" she said.

"Oh. Yeah. 'Loving.' I can hardly read my own writing. 'Loving mother of four eight-week-old kittens, all shots, wormed, flea-dipped . . .'"

"We didn't tell him about the kittens," Jeanette said.

"He'll love the kittens. Let's see . . . 'Winsome. One-year-old—'"

"What's Sparky doing here?" Jeanette asked.

"Mom said she could stay up here till we go to bed. Winsome will be *great* in Leonardo's act, don't you think?"

"Winsome is wonderful," Jeanette said with a smile. There was a sound from under the bed. "What was that?"

"Fraidy's got something under the bed," Bucky said absently. She was still looking over her list. "I think it's a yarn ball. Or maybe a mouse, I don't know . . ."

"Kids?" their father called from downstairs. "Five minutes. We'll be up to kiss you good night."

"Bucky?" Jeanette said.

"What?"

"They'll have a good home with Mr. Leonardo, won't they?"

"Of course!"

"Because that's the most important thing of all."

. . .

The next morning, Bucky raced to the phone before she went downstairs to breakfast. She dialed quickly, getting two sleepy wrong numbers before she reached the number she wanted.

"Bernard? It's Bucky. We'll be at your house right after breakfast."

"Uncle Lenny's still asleep," Bernard said.

"Wake him up. And call Nicholas and Renee and—"

"Aw, wait a minute, Bucky—"

"Okay, okay. Just call Nicholas. We'll call the others. We'll be there in half an hour."

"*Half an hour*? It'll take that long to get Uncle Lenny to open his eyes!"

"An hour then," Bucky said and hung up.

9...

They were all standing in Bernard's driveway, next to his Uncle Lenny's RV.

"Okay, kids, this is The Great Leonardo," Bucky began. "In his regular clothes."

The Great Leonardo's eyes were only half open. He leaned against his RV with his arms folded across his chest.

"Mr. Leonardo, you know me and my sister, Jeanette, and my brother, Harry. These are the rest of our committee — this is Holly from last night . . ."

Lenny Graber sleepily stuck out his hand. Holly giggled and shook it.

"And this is Nicholas . . . This is Marsha . . . This is Renee . . . and Bernard."

"I know Bernard," Lenny said and yawned. "I don't know why we had to do this so early . . ."

"Because we all care so much about the animals," Jeanette said. "And we want to help you with them all we can!"

"Besides," Bucky said, "You'd better start working with them right away if you're going to get your act together. Las Vegas is a long way from Nelkin Falls."

Lenny rubbed his eyes. "Yeah, I guess . . ." he said. "Say, how many are there, anyway?"

"You'll see."

Chuck poked his head out the window of the RV.

"This is Chuck," Bucky said, introducing him.

The kids said, "Hi."

"My mother won't let Chuck stay in the house," Bernard said. "He sleeps in the RV."

Jeanette looked at Bucky. "Won't Mrs. Fishbein let the animals in the house?" she whispered.

"She'll have to," Bucky whispered back. "They can't all stay in there."

"Well, let's go!" Holly said excitedly, and grabbed the door of the RV. The other kids, who had never ridden in one before, cheered and rushed after her.

"Hold it, wait a minute!" Lenny yelled, spreading himself out over the side of the vehicle. "You kids can't all ride in here!" He tapped the iridescent blue-green metal door. "It's got all my costumes and props in the back! It's full of stuff!"

"Well, where do you think we're going to put the animals?" Bucky asked.

"On my silk scarves? In my sawing box? No way."

"I know! We'll put your stuff in the living room, Uncle Lenny," Bernard suggested.

"Your mother'll love that, Bernard . . ."

"My room, then. You can store it there while you're staying with us and then we'll fix up places for the animals in the RV."

Lenny frowned. "Yeah . . . well . . . how many animals *are* there, anyway?" he asked again.

"Let's start getting the stuff out!" Bucky cried, sliding the door open.

"Hey, easy! Eas-y!" Lenny moaned.

. . .

It took them almost an hour to unload Lenny's things because he supervised the carrying and placing of each and every item. When Marsha dropped a box filled with fake birds, Lenny groaned loudly.

"You won't need 'em," Bucky said. "You'll be working with live animals from now on."

"Those feathers . . ." Lenny wailed. "They cost me a fortune!"

But they managed to get everything into Bernard's room with only a slight overlapping into Rhoda's.

"Okay," Bucky said, wiping her forehead with the back of her wrist. "That's everything. Now can we go?"

"They're housebroken, right?" Lenny asked as the eight children piled into the big RV. "And how many are there, anyway?"

. . .

"Stop, stop!" Bucky cried as Lenny braked with a screech. "This is it! This is the shelter!"

"Thanks for the warning . . ." Lenny muttered. "I'll just pull into the driveway . . ." He did, peering at the building through his windshield. "Place could use a coat of paint," he noted.

"It could use more than that," Bucky said.

"Let's go in!" Harry cried. "I want to hold the monkey!"

"Wait a minute, just wait a minute . . ." Lenny turned around in his seat. "I didn't plan on *all* of you trailing after me now . . ."

"We have to go in!" Bucky said.

"Why?"

She thought. "Because we want to," she said.

"Besides, we know Mr. Chesterfield," Jeanette added. "We'll introduce you. He'll want to know who's taking his animals."

Lenny sighed.

"Come on, Uncle Lenny . . ." Bernard pleaded.

"All right . . . Look: I'll take Bernard in with

me . . . and you." He gestured at Bucky. "A bunch of kids would probably make the animals nervous, anyway. I want to see just what I'm getting."

Bucky glanced at Jeanette.

"It's okay," Jeanette said, nodding. "We'll wait outside."

"I want to hold the monkey . . ." Harry protested.

"You will, Harry, you will."

"It won't be too long, Harry," Renee said gently. "Oooh, I can't wait to hold the kittens . . ."

. . .

Bucky and Bernard trotted along on either side of Lenny as they walked up the path. Bucky looked back once and saw Jeanette waggle her fingers in a little nervous wave. Bucky reached over and took Lenny's hand.

"Hey, it's okay, kid. Your hand is sweating. Don't be nervous."

"I just want it to go okay," she said softly.

"It'll go okay. The animals were a good idea. I've been reading all night. Got some great new illusions mapped out." He squeezed Bucky's hand. "Say, how many are there, anyway?"

Mr. Chesterfield was mopping the tiled floor where the animals were kept when they were allowed to walk around. He saw Lenny, Bucky and Bernard through the glass window in the door and came out to greet them.

"Hi, sis," he said, recognizing Bucky.

"Mr. Chesterfield, this is Bernard Fishbein . . ."

"Hi, Bernard."

"—And this is Bernard's uncle—"

"Lenny Graber," Lenny said and shook hands with Mr. Chesterfield.

"He's a magician," Bucky said. "And he wants some nice animals for his act. All you've got."

"Well, just a min—" Lenny began.

"A magician, eh?"

"Yeah, that's right," Lenny said.

Mr. Chesterfield pulled at his mustache. "I never felt right about animals in show business," he said. "Heard some pretty bad stories."

"Not about The Great Leonardo," Bernard said quickly. "No bad stories about him! He loves animals! He's got a duck!"

Mr. Chesterfield frowned. "Heard they drug 'em, beat 'em . . . anything to make 'em perform . . ."

"Oh, no. No," Lenny said quickly. "I'd never do anything like that. Chuck never even had an aspirin! Besides, my animals aren't supposed to perform. *I* do the performing, *I'm* the star . . ." He smiled at the kids, but they were still staring at Mr. Chesterfield, so he cleared his throat and went on. "See . . . the animals, they just get pulled out of hats and baskets . . . They appear inside boxes where they weren't supposed to be . . . You know . . . Illusions?"

"I dunno . . ." Mr. Chesterfield mused.

"Mr. Chesterfield, we're trying to place these animals," Bucky said, spreading her arms. "You sound like you don't want to let them go at all! You don't want to put them to sleep, do you?"

Mr. Chesterfield regarded her, then rubbed his eyes with his thumb and forefinger.

"I'm sorry, sis," he said. "'Course I don't want to put 'em down. I just want to make sure they go to good homes, that's all. I won't let 'em go to someone who's going to mistreat them."

"I'd never let that happen," Bucky said. "Never!"

"What exactly are you looking for, Mr. —"

"Graber. Oh, dogs, cats . . . maybe a monkey . . ."

"Twenty-five dollars apiece," Mr. Chesterfield said. "Donation. Helps pay for upkeep, food, medicine, worming . . ."

Lenny looked down at Bucky, whose mouth was open, and at Bernard, who shrugged.

"Twenty-five d-dollars apiece?" Lenny stammered. "Well, I—"

"Look, Mr. Chesterfield," Bucky interrupted. "The shelter's closing. You said so. You told my mom. The thing is . . . you won't need to buy food or medicine or anything if you get these last animals a home. Mr. Leonardo is going to see that they're well taken care of, aren't you, Mr. Leonardo?" She didn't wait for him to answer. "So couldn't you let him take them off your hands? You know us, Mr. Chesterfield . . . You know my mom and dad. You know we'd never hurt an animal . . . *Please?*" It was a long speech. Bucky was almost panting.

"He's my favorite uncle," Bernard added for emphasis.

10...

The kids were huddled together next to the RV when Bucky, Bernard and Lenny burst through the door with their menagerie and they cheered wildly. Only Jeanette noticed Bucky's downcast face, and ran toward her.

"What is it? Is everything okay?"

The other kids ran for the animals.

"Yeah . . . but he didn't take them all. There are some still left . . ."

"Oh," Jeanette said. "Well, we'll get homes for them, too. Don't worry. Let's see! Let's see what you've got!" She bent down with the other kids and began to pet the animals.

"Well, we've got Winsome," Bucky said,

touching the funny-looking dog with the short legs.

"Awwww!" Marsha sighed.

"And only two of Sweetie's kittens . . ."

Lenny was holding the kittens out to Harry and Nicholas, who were making little cooing noises.

"Why didn't you take Sweetie?" Jeanette asked.

"Leonardo said only two kittens. We left Sweetie to take care of the other two. But he said he had a trick for a big cat . . . so we took Awful."

"Ohhh," Jeanette breathed. Bucky pointed to a cardboard pet carrier. "Well, I'm glad you took him. It would be hard to find him a home the way he is. Now we have time to give him some love and he'll be a star in Mr. Leonardo's act."

"Who's this one?" Renee was already cradling a poodle-mix.

"Zozi," Bucky said. "That's Zozi. She's cute, huh?"

"Yeah . . ." Renee sighed and cuddled the small dog.

"Where's the *monkey*?" Harry cried suddenly.

Lenny opened his work shirt. "Right here," he said with a grin. Cuddles was nestling against his T-shirt.

"Two dogs, two kittens, a cat . . . and a monkey," Marsha counted. "Well, that's a good start, Bucky."

"I guess so," Bucky said.

"I'm not sure about that cat . . ." Lenny said hesitantly.

"He'll be fine, I know he will," Jeanette said. "And he'll love being with you, Mr. Leonardo . . ." She smiled up at him.

"Yeah, well . . ."

Zozi began to yip and Awful hissed inside his carrier.

"Okay, okay, let's all get quiet," Bucky said. "Everyone get in the RV and sit on the floor." They did. "Now," she continued from the door-way, "if we're going to keep the animals calm, *we* all have to be calm." She began to distribute the animals to the kids sitting on the floor of the RV. "Bernard, you take a kitten." He beamed as she handed him a black-and-white one. "And Nicholas, you take the other one."

"What can I take, Bucky," Jeanette asked, holding out her arms.

"You take Awful, Jeanette. You can start loving him right now, but through the holes in the card-board. Holly, you take this—" She handed Holly Winsome's rope leash. "Hold her so she doesn't fall or anything while we're driving."

"Look at her eyes," Holly breathed. "Isn't she the sweetest?"

"What about this one?" Lenny was holding the other rope leash belonging to Zozi.

"Ooooh, let me have her," Renee said, lifting Zozi onto her lap.

Chuck quacked in the driver's seat of the vehicle.

"Hold onto him, Harry," Lenny said warningly. "Keep him away from the others, whatever you do!"

"But I want to hold the monkey!" Harry said.

"I'll keep the monkey in my shirt," Lenny said. "He's scared. You take care of Chuck."

"Okay . . ." Harry pulled the duck onto his lap.

"Ack," Chuck said, as Lenny closed the doors.

"You picked a nice group," Jeanette said to Bucky.

"I hope this works out," Lenny said starting the RV. "Back there in the shelter, I was thinking that maybe just one kitten and the monkey . . ."

"No, no that's not enough!" Bucky said. "*Anybody* can do tricks with one kitten and a monkey!"

"That's easy for you to say, kid." Lenny pulled out onto the street.

A kitten mewed. The kids chorused, "Awww . . ."

"What's that?" Holly asked suddenly.

"What's what?"

"That noise. Listen."

It was coming from the pet carrier. Jeanette bent close to it. "It's Awful," she said. "He's chewing the cardboard."

"Oh, great," Holly said.

"Mr. Chesterfield said Awful was a mean cat.

But I don't think cats can be—OW!" Jeanette shrieked.

"What happened?" Lenny asked.

"Nothing," Jeanette whimpered.

"What is it, Jeanette?" Bucky asked.

"Nothing . . ."

"It is, too. You're bleeding," Bernard said.

"Terrific!" Lenny said to the steering wheel.

"Well, he just got a paw out of the carrier and scratched me a little, that's all," Jeanette said, rubbing her leg. "He didn't mean it . . ."

"Oooooh, it's bad," Holly said, frowning at the scratch.

"Wonderful," Lenny said, throwing back his head.

"It's okay," Jeanette said quickly. "He had all his shots. I won't get rabies or anything . . ."

"We must be almost there . . ." Marsha said nervously.

"*Rowr!*" Awful said from his box.

"He is mean, Jeanette," Nicholas said. "You'd better be careful of him . . ."

"Oh, boy . . ." Lenny muttered.

"He's just fine, Nicholas!" Jeanette insisted. "Just wait until he gets some love, you'll see!"

The scratching noises began again.

"He's going to eat his way out of his box and get us!" Nicholas yelled.

"*ROWR!*" Awful said again and this time the sound was louder.

"Uh-oh, he's got his head out," Jeanette said and scrunched down.

"Hey, you're squashing the kitten!" Bernard cried. "Move back, Jeanette!"

"I can't! There's no room!"

"Come on, Jeanette —"

"*ROWR!*"

"Oh, no! He's out!" Holly cried.

"I'm scared —" Marsha whimpered.

"*Grrrr-rrr-r*"

"Sh, Zozi, sh!"

"*ROWR!*"

"No, Zozi!" Renee shrieked as the little dog jumped off her lap.

"Grab her rope!"

"*ROWR!*"

"Aren't we *there* yet?" Holly wailed.

"Pipe *down* back there!" Lenny called. "How can I drive with all that noise? What's going on, anyw —"

He was interrupted by loud barks, snarls and growls. The sounds filled the vehicle. The kids clung to the walls. Marcia began to cry. Nicholas and Bernard managed to hold onto the kittens, but the other animals were having a free-for-all.

"We're here, we're here!" Lenny cried, and with

a loud squeal, swerved into Bernard's driveway and braked abruptly. It startled animals and children and the fracas stopped.

Lenny leaped out of his seat and threw open the side door.

Renee and Jeanette were nursing scratched arms and legs. Holly was standing up holding Winsome, who was clinging to her, whining. Bernard and Nicholas were hunched over their kittens. Bucky was protecting Harry and Chuck with both arms. Zozi and Awful were glowering at each other in the middle of a wide space the children had made for them.

Lenny looked the scene over. He was breathing rapidly and thinking even more rapidly. I gotta be crazy, he thought. The kid had me sold! Can I think clearly when it's late at night or early in the morning? Look at this mess! What have I done? I gotta be crazy! I don't even have *room* for a bunch of animals —

Suddenly, Awful made a crazy leap for Zozi, who growled and put up her paws in a boxing stance. In a second, they were all flying fur and growls.

"*Hey!*" Lenny screamed. "*Do something, will you?*"

"Get a garden hose, Bernard," Bucky yelled. "Hurry up! The rest of you — don't move!" She hugged Harry, and the duck protested with a loud quack.

"No, no, not that! Don't hose down my van! It isn't even paid for yet! It'll be days before I can move my stuff back into it—" Lenny began to pace back and forth in little steps.

"It'll be days before that, anyway," Holly said from corner. "It stinks in here."

"That's it! That does it! I must have been out of my mind!" Lenny shrieked.

"Get something to throw over them! A blanket!" Jeanette cried. "Oh, hurry, before they really get hurt!"

"What about *us*?" Marsha asked.

Awful leaped onto Zozi's back. Zozi rolled over. Their howling rose to a frightening pitch.

"Hurry! *Hurry!*" Jeanette yelled as Bernard came running with an old beach blanket, which they threw over both animals until they lay still from fear and exhaustion.

Lenny, who had been running back and forth and waving his arms, suddenly slumped to the ground in a heap.

The kids and their charges gingerly climbed out of the RV and stood in the driveway, shaking.

"It's hot under that blanket," Jeanette observed. "We can't leave poor Awful there . . ."

"'Poor Awful,'" Lenny moaned, but no one heard him.

"Well, then we need another box," Bucky said.

"But not cardboard. Harry, run home and get our pet carrier."

"Don't go anywhere without me," Harry cried as he took off.

"Ours is made of Fiberglas," Bucky explained to the slumped heap that was Lenny. "It's chewproof. The thing is, I'm sure my parents won't let you keep it. You'll have to find another one . . ."

"Hold it!" Lenny stood up with his palms raised. "Just hold it. This was a big mistake!"

"But—"

"I mean it! I don't know why I ever let you talk me into this—"

"You said it was a good idea!" Bucky wailed.

"Well, it was, but it's not a good reality." He began to back up. "My van stinks, there's a cat in there that thinks it ought to be 'born free,' a dog that'll never get along with him, and—" He stopped. His eyes widened.

"What is it, Uncle Lenny?" Bernard asked.

Lenny opened his work shirt, which all the children could see was suddenly stained dark blue.

"And a monkey, who just—who just—" Lenny pulled Cuddles away from his body and held her out to Bucky.

"Well, you were yelling," Bucky protested, taking the monkey. "She got scared. What do you expect? *Anybody* could have an accident when she's scared!"

Lenny sighed and shook his head. "Kid, running into you was the biggest accident I ever had. But *I'm* still controlling myself." Bucky opened her mouth, but he held up his hand, stopping her. "I can't do this. I'm sorry, I really thought it would work, but it won't. It *won't*, so don't start talking! Now, everybody. Let's get these animals back into the RV and back to that shelter and that nice old guy with the umbrella over his lip. Come on."

The kids stood there.

"Well," Lenny said, gesturing with his arm, "come *on!*"

"I'm not getting back in there," Marsha said, stepping back.

"Me, neither," Renee said. "I don't want to go through that again."

"We can't take them back!" Bucky cried. "We just can't!"

"It's up to you, kid," Lenny said. "I'm sorry. I really am. I hate to let you down and that old guy, too, but this — will — never — work. I'm here to tell you! Now, I'm perfectly willing to take them all back right now, or else you're stuck with a bunch of — of — well, you're stuck, that's all. I don't even want the duck anymore. I don't think I could ever look at another animal again!"

Bucky looked at Jeanette. "He means it," she said.

Jeanette nodded.

"You better *believe* I mean it! Now what is it? Back to the shelter or you and the animals skip down the yellow brick road on your own!"

"On our own," Bucky said defiantly. "We'll take care of the animals!"

"Bucky?" Jeanette said.

"Here's the carrier!" Harry cried, running up to them.

Bucky took it from him. "Let's get Awful into the carrier," she said. "And then we'll decide what to do."

Lenny sighed heavily. "You're a spunky kid," he said. "What I really should take for the act is *you*. You could make illusions like *no* one would believe!"

"What'll we do, Bucky?" Jeanette asked. "Shouldn't we take the animals back? Where will we keep them?"

"We won't take them back," Bucky said. "Not after all the trouble it took us to get them out."

"Let's take them around the neighborhood," Jeanette said. "We could ask people if they want them."

"We tried that on the phone yesterday," Bucky told her.

"Oh, but once they see them," Renee said, snuggling a kitten, "they won't say no then!"

Bucky stopped. A slow smile crept across the

face. "You're right, Renee," she said. "They can't say no when they see them. You're ab-so-lutely right!"

Lenny looked at Bucky. "You can sell 'em, kid. If anyone can do it, you can . . ." he muttered. "And I'll tell you what I'll do to help you out . . ."

"What?"

"I'll keep the monkey."

"Will you?"

"You'll be good to her?" Jeanette asked. She wasn't sure she trusted him anymore.

"Of course I will!" He took Cuddles gently from Bucky's arms. "You take the duck."

"Oh, yay!" Harry cried.

. . .

"Now. Holly—you want to keep Winsome?"

"For *good*?"

"Well, I meant to take around. But you can have her for good . . ."

"Can't," Holly said. "My parents would flip out."

"Okay. Renee, you want to go with Holly?"

"I want to take Zozi," Renee answered.

"Fine. Marsha, you go with Holly. Nicholas, you go with Zozi and Renee."

"I want my kitten," Nicholas said.

"Okay. Bernard and Nicholas, you go together with both kittens. Oh, boy . . ."

"What's the matter?" Jeanette asked.

"That leaves the two toughest pets—Chuck and Awful." Bucky exhaled loudly. "Jeanette . . . would you take Awful? You're the only one who likes him . . ."

"I'm the only one who's *trying* to," Jeanette said. "Okay. I'll take him. Harry, why don't you come with me?"

"Okay!" Harry agreed happily.

"And I've got Chuck." Bucky sighed again. "Renee, you and I don't have teammates. You want to go with me?"

"Sure, if we can walk the duck and the dog together."

"I think they make a cute couple," Bucky said, looking down at them. "We can try it. Is everyone ready to go?"

"Ready," Holly said.

"All right then. We'll all meet back here—what time is it?"

Nicholas had a Mickey Mouse watch. "One o'clock," he said.

"How much time do we need?" Bucky asked. "Do you think three hours would be enough time?"

"More than enough," Renee said. "I bet they'll take Zozi at the first house we try."

"Be sure to say that all the animals have had their shots," Bucky said. "And that they've been wormed and that they have no fleas, ticks or mites—"

"And tell them to donate something to the shelter if they can," Jeanette finished.

"We'll remember."

"And don't take no for an answer!" Bucky added.

"Back here at four?" Holly asked.

"Back here at four."

11...

"Where are we going first, Jeanette?" Harry asked, grabbing the other half of the pet carrier's handle.

"Let's try houses where we know people," Jeanette said. "That way we can keep track. We want nice people, remember?" She glanced sidelong at the carrier. The top was clear plastic so she could see Awful. He was stretched out on the carrier floor, licking his paws.

"Do you think anyone will really want him?" Harry asked.

Jeanette made a worried face. "I was thinking," she said, "about someone who has a mouse problem. Awful's probably very good at catching mice . . ."

"He's not very nice," Harry said, peering at the cat, who seemed to sneer back at him.

"I keep telling you, he just needs love, Harry," Jeanette said. "He needs someone with patience and lots of love."

"Like Mommy and Daddy . . ." Harry said.

"Like them. Right."

Harry fell silent.

"I know! Let's try the Oglemeyers," Jeanette said after a moment. "They've got a huge yard and a big shed in back on cinder blocks. Bet there's mice there, all right! Remember what Bucky said?"

" 'Don't take no for an answer,' " Harry replied.

"Right. Right," Jeanette repeated. She took a deep breath. "Okay, let's make the Oglemeyers love Awful."

It was a bit of a walk to the Oglemeyers' and Awful seemed to gain weight in his box along the way. They were panting and perspiring as they climbed up the Oglemeyers' porch steps.

Harry knocked twice and Mr. Oglemeyer opened the door. He was carrying a baby.

"Hello," he said. He glanced at the pet carrier.

Jeanette looked at the baby.

"May I help you?" Mr. Oglemeyer asked.

"Uh . . . you have a baby," Jeanette said. "I didn't know you had a baby, Mr. Oglemeyer . . ."

"Memorial Day," he said, beaming. "It'll be memorable, all right. Who are you?"

"Jeanette Muchmore. This is my brother, Harry. We were here with our mother when she sold you blinds last winter. Remember? Only . . . only you didn't have any baby then . . ."

"I remember," Mr. Oglemeyer said.

"Well . . ." Jeanette said, "goodbye."

"Goodbye," Mr. Oglemeyer said, looking puzzled.

"Hey!" Harry blurted. "Don't you want the cat?"

"Cat?"

"It's okay, Harry," Jeanette said, picking up the carrier. "Come on."

"You looking for a home for your cat?" Mr. Oglemeyer asked.

"Yeah!" Harry said. He looked at Jeanette. "'Don't take no for an answer,'" he whispered loudly to her.

"We could use a cat," Mr. Oglemeyer said. "We've got a rodent problem out near the shed . . . and we've been thinking about a nice pet for the baby."

"Well," Jeanette said, "I hope you find one. Come on, Harry . . ."

Harry said, "Jeanette—"

"I don't think Awf—I mean—I don't think this cat would be the right one for you, Mr.

Oglemeyer. Gee, I didn't know you had a baby —"

"What's wrong with him? . . . the cat, I mean?"

"Well, nothing . . . I mean, what he needs is a lot of patience and love and . . . things like that," Jeanette answered.

"Well, we've got lots of that, don't we," Mr. Oglemeyer cooed at the baby. "Let's see this nice kitty . . ." He bent over the carrier. The baby seemed interested, too, looking down and waving its tiny fists. Mr. Oglemeyer lifted the plastic lid. "Hi, kitty-kitty," he whispered softly. The baby gurgled happily in his arms.

"*ROWR!*" Awful shrieked, and clawed at the lid. Mr. Oglemeyer slammed it down and stood up quickly. "Oh, my," he said. They could all hear the hoarse growl in Awful's throat even after they backed away.

"Well, I guess he . . . isn't used to people, is he?" Mr. Oglemeyer said.

"Oh, but he will be," Harry said. "All he needs is love, right, Jeanette?"

"Let's *go*, Harry."

"But 'don't take no for an answer,' Jeanette," Harry whispered again.

"Let's go, Harry," Jeanette said again. He climbed off the porch. "Congratulations on the baby, Mr. Oglemeyer. What's his name?"

"Rebecca," Mr. Oglemeyer answered, smiling.

"I'm sorry about the—" he nodded toward the pet carrier.

"I know," Jeanette said. "If you didn't have Rebecca to worry about, he'd be good for your mice."

Mr. Oglemeyer waved the baby's arm at them as they left his yard.

"'Don't take no for an answer'!" Harry said to Jeanette as they walked. "I thought we were supposed to make them *take* the pet."

"I couldn't let them take Awful in his condition," Jeanette said. "He might've hurt the baby. Look what he did to me." She touched her scratched leg. "The Oglemeyers are nice, but you can't give Awful to a little baby."

"Well, who *can* you give him to?" Harry asked.

.   .   .

"Do you know anyone with a pond?" Bucky asked Renee as they walked together, Zozi trotting at Renee's heels, Chuck waddling from side to side in front of Bucky.

"The Sabatinis made a pond on their property two summers ago," Renee said. "My father worked on the construction, that's how I know."

"Mr. Sabatini? The principal?"

"Uh-huh . . ."

"But he lives way over at the end of town," Bucky complained.

"I know, but where else *would* you find a pond? *In* town?"

"Yeah, right," Bucky agreed. "Okay. Then let's try to find a home for Zozi first, since we're here, where the houses are so close together."

"Aw," Renee said softly.

"Well, you *can* keep her, Renee," Bucky said.

"There's a no-pet clause in our lease," Renee said sadly. "We have a canary but it doesn't sing."

"Then we have to try someone else."

"Oh, okay . . ."

They turned the corner at Town Hall Road and decided to work their way up the block.

"Let's try that house," Bucky said, pointing to a two-story colonial. "They have gardeners working there and we can give Chuck a little sprinkle with the hose."

"Okay."

Chuck led the way up the walk, and Bucky rang the bell.

"No dogs barking inside," Renee observed. "That means they don't have any."

"Yet . . ." Bucky said, tapping her foot.

"Ring again," Renee said. Bucky did. "Hear any footsteps?"

"Nope."

"No one home in there," a voice from behind said. The girls turned around. One of the gardeners was leaning on his hoe and watching them. "They're on vacation. What are you doing with the duck?"

"Trying to find it a home," Bucky answered.

"Oh, yeah? Good luck."

"Thanks." They began to walk back toward the street.

"How about the dog? She need a home, too?" the young man asked as they walked past him.

"Yes . . ."

"Yeah? Well, I'll take her." He tossed his head cockily. "Gimme the leash, I'll take her off your hands."

Renee held Zozi's leash tighter. "No," she said quickly. "You can't have her."

The man shrugged.

"Do you really want her?" Bucky asked.

"Yeah. Sure. Why would I say I did if I didn't?" He shifted the hoe to his other hand. "What else are you giving away?"

"No!" Renee cried. "Come *on*, Bucky!"

"Just a second," Bucky said. She brought Chuck over to the whirling lawn sprinkler and he walked under it, ruffling his feathers.

"Bucky, come *on!*" Renee called again. She had Zozi in her arms.

"I'm coming."

The man grinned at them as they hurried away from the house.

"I wouldn't let him have Zozi," Renee whispered

through clenched teeth. "I hated him. He didn't even pet her or make friends with her or anything. He just wanted her 'cause she was *free*. He'd probably take her and *sell* her to someone or something . . ."

"I thought he was kidding," Bucky said. "He didn't really want her."

"He didn't want her but he would have taken her," Renee said angrily. She was almost in tears. "I didn't like him at all."

"Well, there are lots more houses to try," Bucky said.

"Let's go to the Sabatinis' first," Renee pleaded. "I want to keep Zozi as long as I can."

"Oh, all right," Bucky conceded. "But I think I'll have to carry Chuck. It's too long a walk for him."

. . .

Bucky and Renee took turns carrying Chuck, and Renee had him when they finally arrived at the Sabatinis'.

"Thank goodness we're here," Renee sighed.

"You can put him down now," Bucky said. "And *don't* wipe your face on his back, Renee — uh-oh — "

"What's the matter?"

"That's our car in the driveway," Bucky said.

"In the Sabatinis' driveway?"

"Yeah . . ."

"What would your car be doing in the Sabatinis' driveway?"

"I don't know . . . But if my mom's there, I don't think she'll appreciate this . . ." Bucky said.

"Why not?"

Bucky shrugged. "I don't know . . . It's just that when my parents last heard from me, the animals were all taken care of."

"Oh," Renee said. "Well . . . This is Chuck's last hope, Bucky. The Sabatinis are the only ones we know of with a pond. So we'll have to try. Besides, if you think I'm walking back all that way carrying him—"

"Okay, okay. I wasn't going to go back. It's just a surprise, that's all."

"Well, it's not your fault Mr. Leonardo backed out."

"I know . . ."

"So let's go."

They gave each other nervous looks and headed for the front door. Bucky rang the bell.

"One second!" they heard someone call, and after a moment, Mrs. Sabatini flung open the door. Bucky peered behind her. There was no sign of Mrs. Muchmore.

"Yes?" Mrs. Sabatini said.

Bucky straightened up.

"Hi, Mrs. Sabatini," she said. "I'm Bucky Muchmore. This is my friend Renee—"

"Muchmore! Well, I guess you're looking for your mother."

"No, not exactly," Bucky said.

"No? Because she's here . . . She's in the den. She's been showing me some lovely blinds —"

Bucky nodded. "Blinds," she said, and turned to Renee. "She's demonstrating blinds."

"I heard," Renee said.

"It's okay if you just leave her there, Mrs. Sabatini," Bucky said quickly. "What Renee and I want to ask you will only take a minute."

Mrs. Sabatini looked puzzled. "All right . . ." she said.

"Loretta?" It was Mrs. Muchmore, calling from the den. "I have a marvelous idea! Wait till you see this . . ."

Mrs. Sabatini turned. "Goldie, come on out here for a minute! Your daughter's here!"

Bucky winced.

"My *daughter*?" Mrs. Muchmore appeared in the hall with two sections of blinds in her hands — one light blue, one white.

"*Bucky*?" she said.

"Hi, Mom."

"Hi, Mrs. Muchmore."

"Hello, Renee."

"Mom, do you have business with Mrs. Sabatini?"

"I hope so." Mrs. Muchmore tried to smile at Loretta Sabatini.

"Well, so do I. So how about if I do mine first and then I'll let you get back to yours."

"Okay," Mrs. Muchmore said. "You do yours. I'll wait here."

"Here?"

"Here." She looked at Chuck and Zozi, at Renee and Bucky, then folded her arms.

Bucky sighed. "The thing is, Mrs. Sabatini, we were wondering if you'd like this nice"— she bent down and patted Chuck's head—"duck. For your pond. We knew you had a pond."

"My father worked on it," Renee said proudly.

"A duck for my pond?" Mrs. Sabatini repeated.

"Yes."

"Oh, but"— she turned and smiled at Mrs. Muchmore—"we never filled it."

"Filled what?"

"Filled the pond. With water. We began the construction, but never completed it. We were hoping to get back to it this summer, but things just didn't work out."

"Why do you have the duck, Bucky?" her mother asked.

"Well, we won't, for long," Bucky said quickly. "It's only temporary. So does that mean you don't need a duck, Mrs. Sabatini?"

"I don't remember when I did need a duck, honey."

"Bucky, you also have a dog," her mother said.

"Renee has the dog," Bucky said. "Would you like a dog, Mrs. Sabatini? It has all its shots and it's been wormed and flea-dipped—"

"Thank you, dear, but we already have a dog."

"So I guess . . ." Bucky said, "you won't take the duck . . . or the dog. Right?"

Mrs. Sabatini nodded. "Right," she said. "I'm sorry, dear."

Bucky glanced at her mother. "Well. Okay, then," she said. "Our business is over. You can do yours now. 'Bye, Mom."

"Bev-er-ly . . ." Mrs. Muchmore said as Bucky turned to leave.

"Huh?"

"*Why* do you have the duck and the dog temporarily?"

"Aw . . . Because Bernard's uncle chickened out. Ducked out? Anyway, we thought we'd take them around and find homes for them ourselves."

"What if you don't find homes for them yourselves?" Mrs. Muchmore asked.

"We'll find them. Don't worry, Mom. We'll take care of it — you sell the blinds. The blue ones are pretty, Mrs. Sabatini. They're a nice alternative to drapes and they're energy-saving —"

"*I'll* take care of my business, Bucky, dear," her mother said. "*You* take care of yours."

"I will, Mom. I was only trying to help."

"I know," her mother said. "I know . . ."

. . .

"Why didn't you let your mother drive us back?"

103

Renee grumbled, hefting Chuck again. "It's so far!"

"I didn't want to wait," Bucky said. "She could take forever with one of her demonstrations, and I don't want to lose the time. We need the time, Renee. Chuck's luck might be running out. Do you know of anyone else with a pond?"

"No, Bucky! That's why we came all the way out here! Mrs. Sabatini was the only one! Can't we wait for your mother?"

"No. Let's try this neighborhood. Let's really comb it!"

12...

As four o'clock drew near, the children began to troop back to Bernard's driveway from different directions.

Jeanette and Harry, with Awful still in the pet carrier, were first to arrive. They were followed by Holly and Marsha with Winsome on her leash. Bernard showed up with one of the two kittens. And lastly, Bucky with Chuck and Renee with Zozi.

"Oh, no," Bucky groaned, when she saw the group. "*No* one found any homes?"

"A kitten," Bernard said. "Mr. Oglemeyer took it. He only wanted one."

"For Rebecca. That's perfect!" Jeanette cried.

"Well, at least that's one . . ." Bucky muttered. "Where's Nicholas?"

"He went home crying. He misses the kitten. But he couldn't have kept it anyway. His brother's got white mice."

"No one wanted Winsome?" Bucky asked.

Holly shook her head. "I guess no one wanted Zozi, either."

"No one except Renee," Bucky said. She turned to Jeanette. "I see we've still got the killer."

"He's not a killer," Jeanette said. "He's just not very nice yet. He sure is heavy, though." She rubbed her arms. "How about Chuck?"

"Chuck's heavy, too. And we couldn't find him a pond. The Sabatinis never filled theirs. But guess who was there?"

"Who?"

"Mom."

"Really? What was she doing there? What did she say?"

"She was selling blinds and she wasn't too thrilled. I don't know what we're going to do now . . ."

"Did you ask Mom if we could bring them all home, Bucky?" Harry asked hopefully.

"No, Harry."

"Can anyone keep just one of them?" Jeanette asked the group. "For only overnight?"

Heads shook from side to side.

"Well?" Jeanette turned to Bucky.

"Bernard," Bucky said, "do you think your uncle will keep Chuck for one more night?"

"I'll ask him," Bernard said, and went into the house.

"Oh, please, can I take the kitten?" Harry begged. "I'll keep it in my room. No one will know it's there, I *promise!*"

"Okay, Harry," Bucky said. "We don't have any choice. A kitten is little, so it should be all right. But what about — ?" She waved her thumb at the pet carrier. Awful groaned and stretched. "How about it?" Bucky asked. "Anyone?"

"No way."

"Not me."

"Uh-*uh!*"

"Forget it!"

Bucky made a resigned face.

"He says no," Bernard said, walking toward them. "He says it would only prolong the separation. He didn't want to look Chuck in the eye and tell him he was replaced by a monkey."

"Oh, great," Bucky sighed.

"The shelter?" Marsha offered.

"No!" Jeanette cried. "Oh, no . . . Mr. Chesterfield would be so upset. He thinks the animals have a home. And if we bring them back there . . . They might get put to sleep!"

"She's right," Bucky said. "We don't have any choice. We're going to have to bring the animals home with us."

"Yay!" Harry cheered.

Bucky sighed. "Just for tonight," she said.

. . .

Anyone who passed the group as they trudged along through the residential neighborhood had to smile. Seven youngsters: a kitten draped over a shoulder; a large tiger cat scratching at the walls of his carrier; a small white dog trailing at the end of a leash; a strange-looking mongrel with a head too big for its chunky body and short legs, panting at the children's heels; and a white duck on a rope, leading the way like a fat Pied Piper with wings.

"Are you children having a circus?" Mrs. Warner asked as she wheeled her grocery cart past them.

"Yeah," Bucky moaned, "we sure are . . ."

"We're trying to find homes for them, Mrs. Warner," Holly said. "Do you see anything you'd like?"

"I'd like the duck," Mrs. Warner answered quickly. "Do you know the price of duck these days?"

Holly gasped. "You mean . . . you want to *eat* him?"

"I'm just teasing, Holly," Mrs. Warner said. "Where did you get all these animals?"

The children told their neighbor about the shelter.

"Well, my goodness. Poor Mr. Chesterfield," Mrs. Warner said. "I had no idea."

"How about a dog?" Marsha asked.

"Or a kitten?"

"Or a . . . cat?" Jeanette added, struggling with the carrier.

"I'll talk to my husband about it," Mrs. Warner promised.

"Will you?" Bernard asked hopefully. "Will you? Honest?"

"I will. What a shame about the shelter," she said as she went on her way.

"Boy, I hope she takes one," Bucky said. "She's nice. Mrs. Warner. She'd give it a good home." She looked around. "Did you kids go to that house over there?"

"Uh-huh."

"How about that one?"

"Yup."

"You hit all these houses? And not one sale?"

"The Oglemeyers," Bernard reminded her.

"Oh. Yeah . . ."

As they neared the Muchmores', Bucky sent Jeanette ahead to see if their mother was back yet. Jeanette returned nodding.

"She's in the kitchen," was the report.

"Oh, boy . . ." Bucky said.

"What'll we do?" Jeanette asked.

"I promised Mom we'd have the animals in homes by now . . ." Bucky said, and chewed on her lower lip. "And she doesn't even know how many we've got."

"She won't like it, will she?" Harry observed.

"And what about Sparky?" Jeanette added. "Won't she be upset when she sees all these animals — ?"

"Wait a minute, I'm thinking," Bucky said.

Holly and Marsha sighed and sat down on the curb. Zozi yipped. Awful hissed.

"Come on, Bucky," Marsha said tiredly. "I have to go home soon."

"Okay," Bucky said. "Here's what we'll do: Jeanette and Harry, you go into the kitchen and talk to Mom. The rest of us will bring the animals in through the basement door. We'll take them in one at a time and introduce them to Sparky. That way they can sniff each other's noses the way animals do and they'll be friends. If we can do it quietly, maybe we'll be able to keep them there just for tonight without upsetting the family, and first thing tomorrow — "

" — we start again," Renee said, shaking her head.

"And then we'll have to do something about tomorrow night," Marsha put in.

"They'll all have homes tomorrow," Bucky said firmly. "I'm sure of it."

"That makes one of us," Marsha said.

"Let's go," Bucky said.

Winsome, the sweet clown, went first. The big-headed round-eyed dog was so happy to feel the cool cement of the Muchmores' basement beneath her paws that she ignored Sparky entirely and dropped to the floor panting. Sparky lifted her head in acknowledgment of the new presence and tried to hoist her heavy body to its feet, but gave up with a soft grunt after one try.

One down.

Next came Zozi. Yipping and wagging her stump of a tail, the little white dog pranced over to Sparky and, breathing in tiny snorts, sniffed the pregnant dog all over. Sparky yawned.

"Pet Zozi, Renee," Bucky whispered, "until she falls asleep, too. Now all we've got left are Chuck and Awful."

"The worst!" Holly groaned.

"What about the kitten?" Bernard asked.

"Harry put it in the laundry basket in the garage," Bucky said. "He'll get it up to his room later. Now, which one first?"

"The duck," Marsha said. "He'll be easier than the cat."

They brought Chuck down with Bucky's hand over his beak to stifle his quacks.

"Buck, you can't let them all loose in here like this," Holly said. "They're okay now because they're tired, but pretty soon they'll start to wake up and then what?"

"You're right," Bucky said, "but I think I've got that covered. There's some chicken-wire fencing in back of the compost heap outside and I think what we'll do is make pens for them all out of it."

Marsha said, "Pens?" and giggled. "They'll each have their own rooms. Just like a motel."

"A motel!" Bucky said, grinning. "Right!"

"How can you make a motel without your parents knowing?" Holly asked.

"She can't," Mrs. Muchmore said, clumping down the stairs followed by Harry and Jeanette. "Beverly Muchmore, now you've gone too far."

Bucky glared at her brother and sister.

"It wasn't us, it was the noise!" Jeanette insisted. "You sounded like a parade down here! Harry and I tried to yell over it!"

Mrs. Muchmore surveyed her property.

"I see the duck is still with us," she said, tapping her foot.

"No one has a pond!" Bucky wailed, but Mrs. Muchmore was busy counting.

"You didn't mention the rest this afternoon, Beverly," she said. "Two dogs . . . the duck . . ."

"I really thought the other kids would have found them homes by now. I *did*, Mom . . ."

"What's that?" her mother asked.

"That? That's our pet carrier."

"I can see that. Is there a pet in it?"

"Don't try to touch it, Mrs. Muchmore," Marsha said. "It eats flesh."

"What?"

"It's a cat, Mom, a nice—just a cat."

"Great. Just great."

"It's like a motel, Mom," Bucky said. "They're just checking in for overnight."

"Yes!" Jeanette cried. "A motel for animals! With the very best service . . . The cleanest rags, the nicest leftovers, air conditioning—" She touched the damp stone of the basement wall.

"And little wrapped-up soaps?" Bucky chimed in. "And a Bible in each drawer."

"The trouble with this motel," Mrs. Muchmore observed, "is that animals check in—as they say on TV—but they don't check out."

"They will," Bucky said. "They'll be out first thing in the morning. I promise, Mom, I swear!" She looked at her mother. "Daddy'll have a fit, huh?"

"I can have a fit, too, you know," Mrs. Muchmore said. "And I'm having one! How could you do this? You know what we said!" She leaned against the wall and closed her eyes. "Why me?" she groaned.

"Look, Mom," Bucky said, "if Holly or Marsha or Renee or Bernard or even Nicholas brought home even one animal, their parents would be really mad. I mean, *really* mad."

"You think I'm not mad?" her mother asked.

"No. I know you're mad. But you won't throw the animals out. So I'm risking your mad—for the animals' lives."

Mrs. Muchmore burst into laughter, much to Bucky's relief.

"I may be laughing, but I'm still mad," her mother said. "We told you no more animals and look at this place —" She swept her arm out over the floor. The animals all looked up at her and she made a small whimpering noise.

"We didn't plan this," Bucky insisted. "We really thought they'd all be settled in nice homes by now."

"Just for overnight, Mom . . ." Jeanette pleaded. "You know you can't put them out in the street."

"No, but I can get them right back to Mr. Chesterfield," her mother said. "And that's what we're going to do this minute."

"Oh, no!" Bucky cried. "You can't do that! Mom, you can't!"

"Why not?"

"Oh, Mom —" Jeanette cried, "because Mr. Chesterfield was so glad that they were going with Mr. Leonardo. He'll have to put them to sleep now if we bring them back. We'll never get them out again — only adults can do that . . ."

"So we've got to bring them to the adults. To show them," Bucky said. "Someone will take them — we'll find good homes for them tomorrow — we really will, we've just got to —"

Bernard interrupted her breathless plea. "Besides," he added, "the duck isn't his."

. . .

"Roll out some more wire," Mrs. Muchmore said, two nails sticking out of her mouth. "And be careful you don't cut yourself."

They were just completing a makeshift enclosure for Chuck in the back yard when Mr. Muchmore arrived home. Finding no one in the house, he began to call. They heard him in the back.

"Oh, boy," Mrs. Muchmore muttered. Then she answered, "Out here, dear!"

He stuck his head out the back door.

"Hi!" Mrs. Muchmore said.

"Hi, Daddy!" Harry yelled.

"Hi, Mr. Muchmore," Holly said tentatively. She was the only neighbor left. The others had gone home for supper.

Mr. Muchmore just stared.

"Now, it's not permanent," his wife began.

"It's only for overnight," Bucky added.

"I don't believe it," her father said softly.

"There wasn't any other place," Harry said.

"A duck," his father said, shaking his head.

"They'll be out of here in the morning!" Jeanette cried.

"*They?*"

"There are a few others . . ." Mrs. Muchmore said.

From the basement window, they heard a low growl and then a yelp.

"*Others?*" Mr. Muchmore cried.

13...

They ate scrambled eggs and rye toast for dinner. The children cooked while their mother finished up the pen for Chuck.

"We hoped you wouldn't even notice them, Daddy," Bucky said, salting her eggs for the fourth time. "We thought we'd just put them up overnight and have them checked out before you even knew they were here."

"You thought I wouldn't notice? In our small three-bedroom house, we now have four dogs, four cats and a duck. Not to mention that one of the dogs is about to give birth any second and one cat needs an exorcist more than it needs a home! My basement has been split into barracks with chicken-wire walls, the cement nails you drove in down there are cracking the foundation, *they're* all eating my hamburgers while *I'm* stuck with scrambled eggs, and on top of all that—listen."

They stopped eating to listen.

Awful was yowling and snarling, Zozi was yipping and barking. Outside, the duck was quacking, and upstairs Calpurnia was whining.

"You thought I wouldn't notice," Mr. Muchmore finished weakly.

"Where's the kitten?" Bucky whispered to Harry when dinner was over. "He said 'four cats.' There are really five."

"They never saw the kitten," Harry said. "He's in my room. In my toy box in the closet."

"Okay . . ." she said, "but . . ."

"What?" Jeanette asked. "What's the matter?"

"Nothing," Bucky said. "Just . . . nothing."

.   .   .

That night on her top bunk, Bucky lay on her back with her arms under her head. She knew Jeanette was asleep by the soft steady rhythm of her breathing, and she knew Harry was asleep because Harry always dropped right off. But she wasn't sure about her parents and she wanted to wait until the house was completely dark and quiet. Several times she found herself dozing, but managed to wake up by shaking her head, blinking hard and talking softly to herself.

"It really is my responsibility," she whispered aloud. "I'm the oldest and it's because of me all those animals are downstairs. If they're upset or lonely, it's up to someone to be there to calm them down . . ."

She listened. There was no sound other than the creak of their bed when Jeanette turned over.

Bucky climbed down, tiptoed to the closet where the sleeping bags were kept rolled up and dragged one of them out. Holding it by the strap, she hoisted it over her shoulder and crept quietly down to the basement. Everything was silent until she opened the basement door and turned on the light.

"*Grrrrr-rrrr!*" It was a small dog's tenor growl.

"*WACK!*" from outside.

"SH!" Bucky said, hurrying down the stairs. "Ooooh, sh!" She raced for Zozi and began to pet her. "Quiet, Zozi, it's only me . . . I didn't come to disturb you, I came to make you feel at home . . ." She scratched the little dog's ears and Zozi wagged her tail.

Awful began to pace back and forth in his wired pen like a caged tiger.

"It's okay, Awful," Bucky said. "Everything's okay . . ."

The cat stopped pacing and glared at her.

"Really it is," Bucky said. "You're in a home where there's lots of love. Well . . . Jeanette loves

you . . ." Awful sneered. "And *I* think you're
. . . nice . . ." Awful hissed. "I'd put you in my
sleeping bag," Bucky said, "but I'm afraid you'd
shred it." She left Zozi and went to sit between
Winsome and Sparky so she could pet both of
them at the same time.

"*WACK!*" Chuck said. Bucky could hear him
easily and hoped he wouldn't wake the neighbors.
But then there was another sound.

"Rain," Bucky said out loud. "It's raining."
Winsome looked up at her and the dog's sweet expression made Bucky smile. "I hope it doesn't rain
tomorrow, Winsome," she said. "I don't have a
raincoat for you . . ."

Sparky stirred beneath Bucky's fingers.

"Hi, Spark," Bucky whispered. "Did I scratch
you too hard?"

Sparky grunted.

"Did you make a noise, Sparky?" Bucky said.
"You *never* make a noise . . ."

Sparky made another noise as her body convulsed.

Bucky drew in her breath. Sparky arched her
back. Bucky stared, her eyes getting wider and
wider. Something dark and slick had appeared between Sparky's hind legs.

"Oh . . ." Bucky managed, "oh, my gosh . . ."
She struggled to her feet, tripping over her sleeping
bag in her rush for the stairs. "Oh, my gosh," she
kept repeating as she raced for her room.

"J-Jeanette—Jeanette!" she whispered hoarsely. "Wake up! Wake *up*!"

"Mmm? Huh?"

"Wake up! Sparky's having puppies! Sparky's having puppies!" Bucky flew down the hall to Harry's room and shook his shoulder. "Wake up, Harry! Come downstairs right now!" she said in his ear. "And hurry!"

"Wh-why?" Harry asked sleepily.

"Just do it! And you'll get a big surprise!" Bucky ran back toward the stairs and bumped smack into Jeanette.

"Are you sure?"

"Positive. Come on!"

. . .

Sparky was licking a tiny, black, shiny wet puppy that was almost lost in the pile of rags as Bucky and Jeanette, followed by Harry, crept toward her.

"Will she mind if we watch?" Jeanette whispered.

"No. Just don't make any sudden movements," Bucky said, but she needn't have bothered.

"Oooooh," Harry breathed. "Look . . ."

"Oh, there are two more in the rags, Bucky . . ." Jeanette followed Harry's pointing finger.

"She must've had those while I was upstairs getting you," Bucky said.

"And she'd didn't even cry," Jeanette said in a voice full of wonder.

"Here comes another one! Watch!"

Spellbound, the children watched Sparky's fourth puppy make its appearance in the world. They were so absorbed they didn't hear their mother and father, who had crept to the top of the stairs and were looking down at them.

"Look at her lick them," Jeanette said. "Isn't it wonderful, Bucky?"

"Yeah . . ."

"What's she doing?" Harry asked. "Yuch, what's she *doing*?"

"She's biting off the umbilical cord, Harrison," Mrs. Muchmore said softly. The children looked up, startled, but their parents were smiling.

"It *is* wonderful, Jeanette," Mrs. Muchmore said. "Sparky will handle the whole birth by herself. The cord that she's biting off is what helped the puppies live while they were inside her. That's how they got their food and nourishment. Now they're going to live outside their mother. So they don't need the cord any more."

"How does Sparky know that?" Harry asked.

"She knows," Mr. Muchmore said.

Harry whistled through his teeth. "She sure is smart," he said. "I didn't even know that."

Bucky looked up. "You're smiling, Dad," she said. "Does that mean you're not mad at us any more?"

"I'm smiling at the miracle of birth," her father said. "When it's over, I'll go back to worrying about the four" — he gritted his teeth — "*five* new arrivals and wondering what on earth we're going to do with them!"

"And it'll be at least six weeks for these guys," Mrs. Muchmore added.

"Don't remind him, Mom!" Bucky said.

"Bucky, you children disobeyed us and brought these animals home after I told you not to," their father said, "but I feel good about your caring natures — and the fact that the fate of these animals bothered you so much. Just use some of that caring on your mom and dad next time, will you?"

14...

It was still raining in the morning.

And there weren't five puppies, there were seven.

"You win, Bucky," Jeanette yawned. They had been up all night. "You win the puppy pool. Use it to buy pet food."

"Big deal," Bucky said. "Two dollars. That probably won't even be enough to buy a bag of duck pellets."

"We should have gotten more kids."

"We got everybody we know!"

"We should have asked Mr. Leonardo. And I bet Mom and Dad would've —"

"Never mind. It still isn't enough. And look at the weather. The only one we should take out today is Chuck."

"He's already out," Harry said nervously.

"He's fine, Harry. Ducks are supposed to get wet."

"I want him in here," Harry complained.

"Harry, he needs the water," Bucky said. "He'd be swimming now if we'd found him a pond."

"Swimming is better than standing around in the rain," Harry said. "I'm going to check him again." He went outside.

"Look at that," Jeanette said. "It's a regular tornado."

"Boy, it's gonna be fun out there today," Bucky said, making a face. "I wish we could find a way to make the people come to us instead of us dragging the animals around outside in this weather—"

"Oh, yeah, that'd be nice," Jeanette said.

"Yeah . . ." Bucky said. Her eyes began to glaze and she stared blankly at the basement door until Harry slipped back in.

"Oh, Harry, you got soaked," Jeanette sighed. "Look at him, Bucky, he—" She stopped when she saw Bucky's expression. "What's the matter now?" she asked.

"Sh," Bucky said, still staring straight ahead. "I think I'm getting an idea . . ."

"Buck?" Harry said.

"Just a second, Harry. Listen, Jeanette, what do you think of this?"

"Buck?"

"Just a second, Harry," Jeanette said. "What? What's your idea?" She leaned in toward her sister.

"Buck?"

"We can do it. We won't have to walk anywhere. We can stay in one dry place."

"Buck?"

"How?" Jeanette asked. "How can we stay in one dry place?"

"Buck?"

"What *is* it, Harrison?"

"Chuck is fine."

"I *know* that—"

"But there's something in there with him."

"In where?"

"In the pen. Eating. From that bowl of bread and milk we left out there."

Bucky frowned. "Well, what is it?"

"I don't know," Harry replied.

"Come on, Bucky," Jeanette said, opening the door.

"We'll get soaked. Look at Harry's pajamas!" Bucky wailed.

"So what? It's warm out. We'll change when we get back in. Let's see what's eating Chuck's bread."

They held some newspapers over their heads and ran out to the back yard.

Hunched over the duck's bowl was a prickly-looking ball.

"It looks like my Nerf," Harry said, "but it's eating."

"What is it?" Jeanette asked.

Bucky shrugged. "I don't know," she said, "but it's another animal."

"It must've heard about the motel," Harry said.

"How did it get in there?" Jeanette wondered. "Oh, I see!" She pointed. "It dug under the chicken wire. See? There's a hole right there." She crept closer.

"Don't touch it," Bucky warned. "Maybe those prickly things stick. Like cactus."

"Let's go ask Mom what it is," Harry said. "I don't want it to hurt Chuck." The duck, however, was paying the newcomer no attention.

The children ran for the house. "Boy," Bucky muttered to herself. "Now we've got five cats, eleven dogs, a duck . . . and a stinger ball."

. . .

"It's a hedgehog," Mrs. Muchmore said. "And you don't have to find a home for it. It's wild."

"Will it hurt Chuck?" Harry wanted to know.

"I think it only wants to eat," Mrs. Muchmore said. "Which is what you kids had better do. And after that, I just don't know . . . You can't go peddling animals door-to-door in this weather . . . ." She sniffed the air. "Terrific," she said.

127

"We're turning into Noah's Ark. Noah and his family must have worn clothespins on their noses for forty days and forty nights."

"You haven't heard my idea," Bucky said.

"I don't want to," Mrs. Muchmore said.

"No, this is a good one. Listen."

· · ·

It took almost two hours to make the arrangements. Bucky did the calling and Jeanette and Harry painted signs. By eleven o'clock, they were all at the shopping center: the three Muchmores, Bernard, Holly, Marsha, Renee, Nicholas, Awful, Winsome, Zozi, Chuck and the kitten. Only Sparky, the puppies and the hedgehog were still at home.

"No one's seen the kitten yet," Harry remarked to Bucky. "We could probably keep him."

"Well, we need him to show," Bucky said. "Kittens are cute. People will want to hold him and then we can make our speech while they all fall in love with him."

"Are you sure Mr. Safer will let us use his place?" Holly asked. She was juggling signs under her arm.

"He said we could stand right under his awning. As long as we don't block the entrance, he said it was all right. The rain is letting up anyway."

"Where should we put these signs?"

"Sit, Zozi," Renee said. "Look! Look everybody, she *sat*! When I told her to! Isn't she the smartest?"

"Sit, Winsome," Holly said, but Winsome only made a little howling noise in her throat and wagged her tail.

"Well, at least she's got pretty eyes," Holly said.

Bucky was busy standing her signs up against the wall.

"They're good," Bernard said.

"Thanks," Jeanette said with a smile.

"'The Nelkin Falls Shelter is in trouble,'" Marsha read out loud. "'We need YOU to help.'"

Renee read another sign. "'We need donations. We need loving people to adopt the pets or they'll all die.' Gee, Jeanette, do you think you should have said that?"

"Yes," Jeanette said firmly. "That may wake people up. No one wants animals to die."

Mr. Safer came out of his store and smiled at the wet-looking group.

"Hi, kids," he said, and looked down at the animals. "They're cute. Awww . . . kitten . . ." He went to Harry and stroked the little fur-ball in his arms.

"Told you," Bucky said.

"Well, I hope you get some good responses,"

Mr. Safer said, stepping back into his card shop.

"Thanks for letting us use your shop, Mr. Safer," Bucky said.

"That's all right. I'm glad to help."

"And it's good public relations," Holly whispered to Bucky when he'd gone inside. Holly's father was in public relations.

"Well, look at this, look at this," a balding man in a raincoat said, smiling. "Aren't you kids something, aren't you something!"

"We are, we are," Marsha said and Bucky jabbed her in the ribs.

"Do you want an animal, sir?" Bucky asked. "Would you like to make a donation?"

"This is great, just great," the man said, nodding. Then he walked away.

"Wonderful, wonderful," Holly sighed.

"Hey, everybody!" Bucky shouted to people hurrying in and out of stores and to and from their cars in the parking lot. "Hey! *Hey*! Come over here! Come see what's happening in Nelkin Falls! Pretty soon you won't have an animal shelter! Pretty soon you'll have a lot of stray animals roaming around! They'll get in your garbage! They'll wreck your lawns! They'll dig up your bushes! And these animals right here — these animals will all have to be put to sleep! And it'll be *all your fault*!"

Some shoppers hurried by. Some smiled and

continued on. But Bucky's speech worked. People came over to them. Soon, someone was holding the kitten. Someone was petting Zozi. Winsome's front paws were on someone's knees. Someone was even feeding Chuck.

Bucky continued to talk and point to the signs.

"Is this kitten free?" a woman asked.

"Yes, Ma'am, they all are," Bucky told her. "They've all had their shots and everything."

"Well, land's sake," the woman said.

"Does anyone have a pond?" Bucky called to the crowd. "Ducks are great with ponds . . ."

A young man stepped over to Renee. He was tanned and muscular. Renee peered into his face, then drew in her breath. He smiled.

"You're the kid givin' away animals," he said.

"You're the gardener," Renee said.

"See? We're old friends."

"No, we're not . . ." Renee said.

"Still got that dog, I see," the man said, nodding at Zozi.

"Yes . . ."

"Well, I'm gonna take her," he said.

"No, you can't —" Renee said. Tears welled in her eyes. Zozi wagged her tail. Renee picked her up.

"Oh, yeah?" the young man said. He was frowning now. "Does that sign say you want these animals to have homes or not?"

"*Good* homes," Renee said.

The young man snorted. "I got a good home. Listen, the kid over there said they'd be put away if no one took 'em, didn't she? Well, I'm takin' one."

"You can't just take one!" Renee wailed, blinking back tears. "You have to — sign a paper first. You have to prove you'll give her a loving home —" She hugged Zozi tighter and the dog licked her face. "Bucky!" Renee called.

Bucky turned. "What?"

But Renee could only point, first to the man, then to Zozi.

Bucky came over.

"What is it?"

"He wants Zozi. The gardener . . ." Renee said and began to cry loudly.

"Well?" Bucky said.

"Hey," the young man said with a sneer. "You want the dog taken or not? This stuff all baloney or what?" He flicked his fingers at the sign. The knot of people had stopped talking to listen.

"No, it's not baloney," Bucky said. "But the pets have to have a good home. Or we don't let them go."

"Yeah, so what makes you kids think it won't have a good home?" the man grunted.

"Bucky —" Renee began.

"Renee, will you keep Zozi?" Bucky asked.

Renee cried even louder. "I argued with my

parents all night over Z-Zozi—" she sobbed. "But our lease won't let us and my mother says we can't move."

"Well, what do you say, huh?" the young man said, holding out his hand for Zozi's rope leash.

"He won't—he won't be kind to her," Renee stammered. "He didn't even ask any questions about her . . . What she's like, or her medical history, or what she eats or—"

Bucky made up her mind. She stuck out her jaw. "You can't have her," Bucky said.

"You hear that?" the man said, turning to the small crowd. "She'd rather have the dog put away!"

"I would not," Bucky said, also to the crowd. "But we won't let them go to just—just *anyone!*"

Bernard moved toward Bucky and the young man.

"Why do you want this dog, sir?" he asked politely.

"What's it to ya? I like dogs. I'm an animal lover." He grinned at the crowd.

"You really like animals?" Bernard asked.

"Yeah."

"Do you believe," Bernard asked seriously, "what people say about pets and their owners? That lots of times they're alike? Sometimes they even look alike?"

The young man frowned. "So?"

"We try to match up our pets with the right

owners," Bernard said, staring up at the man earnestly. "And if you really like all animals, I think I have the right pet for you."

"What is it?" the man asked suspiciously.

"Oh, a pussycat, of course," Bernard answered. "A nice . . ."—he reached for Awful's pet carrier—". . . friendly, cuddly pussycat." He held the carrier as high as he could so the young man could study Awful through the plastic lid.

"Uh, Bernard, can I talk to you for a minute?" Bucky said, grabbing his arm.

"Certainly," Bernard said. "My associate and I will have a conference while you study this fine animal," Bernard said as he handed the carrier to the young man and stepped off to the side with Bucky.

"You want to give him Awful?" Bucky whispered. "Are you kidding? Awful gets mad if you even *talk* to him!"

"So does this guy," Bernard answered.

Bucky grinned a slow grin. "You think it's a good idea?"

Bernard grinned back. "I think it's one of my best," he answered.

"Well, we can't give him the carrier," Bucky said. "My father'd just have a fit. It's ours and it's expensive. And if he ever took Awful out of it, he'd know right away we sent him up the river."

Bernard frowned and thought.

"I think you have to sacrifice the carrier, Bucky," he said.

"Okay," Bucky said. "I'll risk it with my dad. Let's go tell him we'll throw the carrier in with the deal." They turned around and stared open-mouthed. The carrier, with the lid open, was on the ground. The young man, whose face had softened so that they hardly recognized him, was holding Awful in his arms. He was nuzzling his nose in Awful's fur.

He looked up. "I like him," the man said.

The kids stared at each other.

"I'd like to take him. Is it okay?"

The kids stared.

"Hey! You!" He indicated Bucky with a nod of his head. "Can I take this cat or not? What's he like to eat?"

Bucky blinked.

"Uh — well, he likes canned liver . . . Gee, he — he likes you!"

"Yeah . . ." The young man smiled. His eyes smiled, too, this time. "What's his name?"

"Awf —" Harry began, but Bucky clapped her hand over his mouth.

"Lovey," Bucky answered. "His name's Lovey. You pet him while I get you a box . . ."

"I don't need a box," the man said. "I'll carry him like this." He cradled Awful against his shoulder.

"Mister," Bucky said, "you've got yourself a cat."

"Listen," the man said. "He's purring."

Bucky nodded. And kept nodding.

The young man walked away, with Awful looking over his shoulder at the kids.

"Do you believe *that*?" Jeanette said.

"Uh-uh!" Renee said. Her tears had dried on her face and streaked it. "I never saw anything like that in my life."

"Well," Bernard said, casually, "it was easy to see those two were a perfect match." He breathed on his knuckles and wiped them on his shirt in self-congratulation.

"Gee, Bernard, you're a genius," Bucky said.

"And you saved Zozi," Renee added. "I think he would have been just terrible with Zozi—"

Just then, Mr. Safer came out of his store.

"Okay, everyone," he said loudly. "This is Mr. MacMurphy from the *Nelkin Falls Trader*. He's going to take your pictures, so everybody *smile!*"

A flash went off. Kids and animals blinked.

"What's this all about?" Bucky asked.

"I thought it'd make a good story, what you kids are doing," Mr. Safer said. "Now, Mr. MacMurphy, come right out here . . . That's right, under the awning . . . No, stand here, so I can put the kid with the duck right under where it says 'Safer's Stationery.' That's it. Okay, everybody, get around the kid with the duck and *smile!*"

Flash!

"Great. Great picture," Mr. Safer beamed.

"Mr. MacMurphy," Bucky said, "are you going to write something about the closing of the shelter?"

15...

By five-thirty all the kids had left was Chuck.

Winsome had gone with some beaming newly-weds who'd just moved into the Nelkin Falls Garden Apartments not far from the shopping center. They'd left their name and number with Bucky and promised to send a donation to the shelter.

Zozi had gone with the woman who'd been interested initially in the kitten. She had decided Zozi's little loud yips would make her the perfect watchdog for a widow living alone. Renee had cried all over again, but the woman had offered to let Renee visit and have a job walking Zozi if she liked.

And Mr. MacMurphy had taken the kitten.

"Wasn't that great?" Bucky said to her friends as she collected the signs. "Don't you feel good?"

"All the animals got nice owners," Renee said. "I feel good about that."

"Do you think Mr. MacMurphy will really write about us in the *Trader*?" Marsha asked.

"I think he'll write about the shelter, that's the important thing," Bucky said.

Harrison bobbed up and down excitedly.

"We did just what we told Daddy we'd do," he said. "We got all our animals placed today!"

"Except Chuck," Jeanette reminded him.

Bucky said, "We can't count Chuck because he wasn't in the shelter to begin with. And now that we've done it—we can go back and get the rest of the animals! Here, Harry." Bucky handed him the duck's rope. "I'll take the pet carrier . . . Let's go home."

. . .

Mr. Muchmore heard the commotion as soon as he opened the front door.

"Don't pick it up so high! Sparky growls when you do that!"

"But I want to see if it's a boy or a girl!"

"It's too early to tell! Put it down, Harry!"

"It is *not* too early!"

"Bucky, don't sit! There's a puppy under you!"

"Sparky's going to bite you, you'll see . . ."

"Sparky doesn't know how to bite —"

Mr. Muchmore put down his briefcase. "Hello, I'm home, oh, hi, Dad, hello, dear . . ." he mumbled.

"Hello, dear," his wife said. "Why are you standing here talking to yourself?"

"Because no one seems to notice when I come home, that's why."

"I notice." She kissed him. "The kids placed all the animals today."

"They did? Really?"

"Well, except the duck. And Sparky's puppies, of course."

"We still have the duck?"

"And the hedgehog."

"*What* hedgehog?"

"Well, he doesn't count. He checked in on his own."

"Credit card, I take it . . ."

"It's the American way. I think you should congratulate the kids. They did a marvelous job. You can read about it in tomorrow's *Trader*."

"They're in the paper?" he asked.

"They will be. In the 'Town Folks' section. Pictures and everything. A Mr. MacMurphy called a while ago to interview me."

"You?"

"He wanted you, too, but you weren't here. I told him not to bother you at work."

"Oh, you did, eh?"

"Yes . . . but I mentioned your name."

"Thanks a lot." He smiled. "Well . . . I am glad they're all gone. I think we would have needed a whip and a chair for that cat."

"Funny about that cat . . ."

"Dad!" Bucky came up from the basement. "Hi! We got all the animals homes —"

"I just heard. Congratulations. I'm proud of you, Buck."

Bucky grinned and blushed. "Good," she said. "I deserve it. We still have the duck, though . . ."

"I know. I think I'll drive him up to the lake area over the weekend. There's a kids' camp there . . . I think they'd like to have him."

"Great," Bucky said.

"And guess what happens after dinner?" her mother asked.

"What?"

"Why, Bucky, I'm surprised at you. An experienced motel owner like yourself?"

"What do you mean?"

"What happens when a guest checks out of his room?"

"He brings the key to the desk?"

"What else?"

"He pays his bill?"

"Yes . . . but what do the motel people do?"

"They say, 'Thank you, come again'?"

"After that."

"Uh . . ."

"Beverly . . ."

Bucky wrinkled her nose. "They clean the rooms and make the beds."

"Bingo," her mother said.

16...

The Muchmores had the *Trader* story mounted, framed and hung on their living room wall.

There was a picture of Jeanette and the duck under Mr. Safer's awning.

There was a picture of Bucky and the widow holding Zozi.

At the bottom there was a row of pictures of all the signs.

And there was a picture of Mr. Chesterfield in front of the shelter, showing the paint peeling off the stucco walls.

The headline said: NELKIN FALLS' KIDS CARE.

The Muchmores' phone rang all morning. The neighbor kids called. Their mothers and fathers called. And Mr. Chesterfield called. After she had hung up, Mrs. Muchmore assembled her children in the kitchen.

"Mr. Chesterfield has invited you to come down to the shelter," she said.

"What for?" Jeanette asked.

"He'd just like all of you down there. Can you round up the others?"

"Sure," Bucky said, "but didn't he say why he wanted to see us?"

"Not exactly," their mother answered, "but he sounded as if he were crying."

. . .

They could hardly fight their way through the crowd of people when they arrived at the shelter, but someone recognized them and the crowd parted to let them in.

"What's going on?" Holly asked, bewildered.

Bucky shrugged. "I don't know, but Mr. Chesterfield asked for us, so let's find him." She called out, "Mr. Chesterfield? *Mr. Chesterfield?*"

"Sis? Is that you? Come on back!"

They pushed their way toward each other.

"Here they are! Here are my wonderful kids!" Mr. Chesterfield grabbed as many of them as he could in his arms. Jeanette giggled as his mustache brushed against her cheek.

"You should have brought the animals back

when the magician backed out," he said, "but I'm sure glad you didn't. You see all these folks? They saw you at the shopping center—they read about you in the paper—now, look—" He pulled the shirt sleeve of a man near him. "This is Tom. He's volunteering his time to paint the place. The whole place! And these—" He touched some more sleeves. "These fellows are going to help him. This lady—she's going to start a committee to raise funds. Perpetual funding of the shelter. The town's taking it over, going to run the shelter itself. Pay my salary, keep the place going. The high-school principal—he's going to put the shelter on the school's Help Program. Kids'll come down here every day, learn about animals, help take care of them, learn to dispense medication, give shots—"

"Gee, that's wonderful, Mr. Chesterfield," Bucky said.

"And—and Jenkins? the nursery man? He's going to landscape the outside. We're going to build a nice run for the dogs, an area for the cats—and it's all because of you kids. You kids . . ."

Embarrassed, they grinned at each other and looked at the floor.

"And now, I'll be able to take those puppies off your hands," Mr. Chesterfield finished.

"Oh," Jeanette said and stuck out her lower lip.

"Let's have a big cheer for the kids!" Mr. Chesterfield called.

"Hip, hip —"

"*HOORAY!*" the crowd yelled.

"What did Mr. Chesterfield say?" Harry asked.

"Hip, hip —"

"*HOORAY!*" the crowd yelled.

"He's taking Sparky —" Jeanette whimpered.

"Hip, hip —"

"*HOORAY!*" the crowd yelled.

Harry and Jeanette burst into tears.

.   .   .

Lenny Graber steered his RV down Hibernia Street and rounded the corner onto West Beach. He drove slowly because he found it made Cuddles nervous if he swerved sharply. Next to him on the front seat was a rolled-up copy of the *Nelkin Falls Trader* with the article about the shelter on the front page.

"Boy," Lenny muttered to himself as he glanced at the paper. Inside his shirt, Cuddles chattered nervously and Lenny stroked her.

"Oh, boy," he said again as he noticed Bucky standing at the curb, her arm around her sister. Lenny pulled up into the driveway next to them.

"Hey!" he called, sticking his head out the window.

"Oh, hi, Mr. Leonardo," Bucky said. "Where are you going?"

"Vegas," Lenny answered. "We're finally on our

way. Me and my baby." Cuddles chattered again. "Say, this place looks familiar . . ."

"It's the shelter," Harry blurted. "Don't you remember?"

"Oh. Yeah," Lenny said. "Well, it *was* a little early in the morning for me. And speaking of the shelter, I caught your little write-up in the local rag—" He glanced down at the paper on the seat beside him.

"It wasn't little," Harry said, "it was big."

"Yeah, Harrison Watt, it was big, now you mention it. There was even a picture of my duck!"

"It isn't your duck," Bucky said.

"The duck gets in the papers and I don't," Lenny complained.

"You could've helped . . ." Bucky said.

"I'm the one who needs the publicity," Lenny told her.

"What you need is a new act," Bucky said.

"I made you an offer, kid—you wanna be in it?"

Bucky laughed. "Listen," she said, "the shelter's going to stay open now. So if you really don't want the monkey—"

"If I don't want the monkey!" Lenny interrupted. "Are you kidding?" He gently lifted Cuddles out of his shirt and held her up. Harry clapped his hands together delightedly. "Are you kidding?" Lenny repeated. "I *love* this monkey. You couldn't pry us apart!" To prove it, the monkey reached out and put her small arms around Lenny's neck. "See?" he said, beaming.

"I hope you'll both be very happy," Bucky said.

Lenny revved the engine. "We will," he said. "And we'll be successful. I'll send you passes to my show."

"I'll be waiting at the mailbox," Bucky said.

"So long, kid. So long, Harrison Watt. And so long, Janet."

"Jeanette," Bucky corrected.

"Right." He tucked the monkey back in his shirt.

"'Bye, Cuddles!" Jeanette and Harry called.

"So long, The Great Leonardo," Bucky said softly as Lenny pulled away.

Jeanette began to whimper again.

"Come on, Jeanette—" Bucky said.

"Aw, but, Bucky—I wish Mr. Chesterfield didn't have to take Sparky and the puppies. We wanted to keep her from the beginning, remember?"

"I know, but then it was the shelter animals who needed our help. And we gave it. And it all turned out okay. Sparky will be fine now and that's the main thing."

"But what about our motel?" Harry asked. "We cleaned it all up and we still have the pens built . . . We're all ready for new guests now!"

"The shelter's a nicer place, Harry," Bucky said. "We can bring our stray animals there. Mr. Chesterfield won't have to put them to sleep now.

He'll have lots of room for them. And we've still got Calpurnia and Ruby and Opal and Fraidy —"

"And the hedgehog," Jeanette added.

"Yeah, and the hedgehog. And we can always visit Zozi and Winsome and the kittens —"

"And Awful," Jeanette said.

"Maybe," Bucky said.

"And we've got something else, too," Harry said.

"What?"

"Well, remember when Jeanette and I were crying before?"

"Uh-huh."

"And remember the people started to laugh and pat us on the back and cheer us up and everything?"

"Uh-huh."

"And remember when Mr. Chesterfield held my hand and led me away for a private talk?"

"Uh-huh."

"Well, he gave us a reward."

"He did?"

"Yup."

"Well, what did he give us?"

Harry opened his fishing jacket. Four long white ears poked out at his neck.

"*Rabbits?*" Bucky screamed.

"Two!" Harry beamed. "A boy and a girl!"

"Oh, Harry!" Jeanette cried.

The rabbits nuzzled Harry's neck and each other.

"A boy and a girl . . ." Bucky said to Jeanette. "Boy and girl bunnies."

"Oh, Bucky," Jeanette said with a smile. "Do you think they'll have babies?"

. . .

Mr. and Mrs. Muchmore stood in the doorway of their daughters' bedroom. They were looking at Bucky and Jeanette, illuminated by the light from the hall.

"They certainly look innocent when they're sleeping, don't they?" Mrs. Muchmore whispered.

"They certainly do . . ."

She smiled at him. "They're cute rabbits, Howard . . ." she said.

"Are you sure they're outside?"

"The rabbits? Of course I'm sure. They're in the duck's pen. The kids are going to build a hutch — that was the deal, remember?"

"I remember," Mr. Muchmore said, "but I was thinking that maybe Bucky brought them in to sleep with."

"Oh, Howard . . ."

"She's something, that one. You know what she did?"

"What?"

"She gave me the two dollars she won in the puppy pool. To buy lettuce. For the rabbits."

"Awww, Howard . . . Did you take it?"

"Of course!"

They laughed softly and moved away from the door.

"They're never going to stop bringing animals home," Mrs. Muchmore said. "But that's because they know us."

Mr. Muchmore sighed. "Rabbits. Ducks. Dogs. Cats. Hedgehogs . . . Come on," he said, taking his wife's arm. "Let's go look at Harry."